The Magic Gifts

The Magic Gifts

Sinéad de Valera

Foreword by Síle de Valera

WOLFHOUND PRESS

First published in 2000 by
Wolfhound Press Ltd
68 Mountjoy Square
Dublin 1, Ireland
Tel: (353-1) 874 0354
Fax: (353-1) 872 0207

The Arts Council
An Chomhairle Ealaíon

Wolfhound Press receives financial assistance from The Arts Council/An Chomhairle Ealaíon, Dublin, Ireland.

British Library Cataloguing in Publication Data
A catalogue record for this book is available from the British Library.

ISBN 0-86327-822-1

10 9 8 7 6 5 4 3 2 1

The stories included in this book originally appeared in *The Four-Leaved Shamrock and Other Tales*; *The Magic Girdle and Other Stories*; *The Miser's Gold and Other Stories*; *The Verdant Valley and Other Stories*; *The Emerald Ring and Other Irish Fairy Tales*; and *Fairy Tales of Ireland*.

Cover Illustration: Aileen Johnston
Illustrations: Tana French
Cover Design: Wolfhound Press
Typesetting: Wolfhound Press
Printed and bound by MPG Books Ltd., Bodmin, Cornwall

Contents

Foreword

Sinéad de Valera was often viewed as a quiet, diminutive, compliant woman on the arm of a man who literally over-shadowed her. The truth was very different. She was intelligent, strong-willed and independent and had an enduring influence on those she met. She had many deep and lasting friendships with people of widely differing political and religious views. Through her long life, she had opportunities to meet with men and women of influence throughout the world; but children were always her abiding interest and concern.

The imagination of a child is a fertile place, always seeking novelty and adventure. Sinéad de Valera delighted in these qualities, which sparked off stories in her mind with which to further entertain her young audience. She was a person with that rare gift of being able to communicate with children without ever being condescending. Children always appreciated this and sought her company. She was particularly aware of vulnerable children, vulnerable due to either intellectual capacity or economic circum-stance. I remember her saying that teaching a slower pupil was the test of a good teacher; anyone could teach a bright child!

As a teacher herself, she always believed that any good story should have a moral. Perhaps this is one of the reasons why fables and folk-tales always appealed to her. This volume includes four stories — 'The Well at the World's End', 'The Wig and the Wag', 'Eagle and Angel' and 'Ashapelt' — which are of particular interest to the folklorists. These stories were told to Sinéad's mother (born 1839); she in turn recounted them to Sinéad, who faithfully recorded them. When folklorists were first made aware of these stories, in the 1930s, they alluded to the fact that these were the first folk-tales recorded from Fingal, Co. Dublin.

Sinéad de Valera was a fervent nationalist and had an abiding interest in Irish history and the Irish language. In her stories she wished to portray the lives of her characters in an Irish context. As she was a member of the Gaelic League and knew many of the well-known literary figures of the time, this should not be too surprising.

Over the years there has been reference to Sinéad's love of the stage. She was considered to be quite an accomplished actress in her day. She took part in a number of productions, of which the most famous was *The Tinker and the Fairy* with Douglas Hyde. She also wrote plays for children, in both Irish and English, and took great joy in attending rehearsals and productions of these plays. Many of the children who took part in them have told me of their happy memories of her attendance at these performances and that these memories have remained with them through adulthood. Indeed, I remember that she was always there, sitting in the front row, at my school plays.

It is more important than ever that young people should learn the value of books at an early age, particularly with the enormous growth in technology. Computers can be a tremendous aid to education, but they can never be a substitute for the journey through the imagination provided by a well-written book — a journey that is better still if there are books available that give the opportunity for such exploration in a cultural setting to which we can immediately relate.

Bedtime stories are an age-old custom, and Sinéad, having had seven children of her own, decided, like other mothers before and since, to continue entertaining many generations of children by writing these stories down for them to enjoy. They are compact and of just the right duration for such a purpose. Many people, over the years, have asked me where they could find a volume of Sinéad de Valera's books, as they enjoyed them as children and wished to obtain copies, not just for nostalgic reasons, but to read them to their own children. This is an excellent presentation, which I can warmly recommend, of some of Sinéad de Valera's work.

I hope that those children of this generation who either read these tales themselves or have them read to them will glean from them the joy and pleasure that I did when I was a child.

Síle de Valera
Minister for Arts, Heritage, the Gaeltacht and the Islands
September 2000

The Magic Gifts

Once upon a time, and a very good time it was, there was a poor widow who had a son named Jack. Jack was a good boy, but he was very simple and had not much sense. The mother found it hard to get food and the other necessaries of life for herself and her son. So Jack at last made up his mind to go and seek his fortune.

After walking for miles and miles, he came to a farmer's house. The farmer and his wife made him welcome and gave him a good supper. When he had eaten enough they all sat around the fire and talked. Jack was astonished and shocked to hear the farmer and his family boasting of the way they had cheated and tricked their neighbours, but when he went to bed he thought no more about it.

Early the next morning he left the house, and the farmer's wife gave him a griddle cake to eat on his journey. Toward evening he came to a large green. In the centre of the green there was a huge clump of furze covering a rock.

As he came nearer, Jack was surprised to see that the rock was scooped out so as to make a neat little dwelling-house. The front of the house was white-washed and the thatched roof looked as if it had been freshly put on. A nice old woman was leaning over the half-door. Jack wished her good evening.

The woman, smiling kindly, returned his greeting and asked if he would like to rest for the night at her house. 'You must be tired after walking all day,' she said.

Jack said he would be delighted, and after he had enjoyed a good supper the woman told him that, if he wished, he could remain in the house and help to mind the cows and goats and hens and to keep the bit of land in order.

He agreed to this. He worked well, and the woman was very kind to him. After three months had gone by, she suggested that he should go home to see his mother. The old woman said he could return to her house whenever he wished.

Jack was pleased with this arrangement and when he was leaving the old woman gave him a hen, which she said would serve as wages for his work.

'Bring the bird to your mother,' she said, 'put it on the table and give it some oats. Then say, "Hen, hen, lay your eggs," and you'll see something that will surprise you.'

Jack thanked the woman and went off with the hen. He came to the house where he had stayed before and they gave him a great welcome and invited him to spend the night there.

After he had eaten his supper, Jack and the family sat around the fire and talked.

'How did you get on since you were here before?' they asked him.

Then Jack told them of his work and how the old woman had given him a hen for his wage.

'However,' he added, 'maybe it's a good bargain, because she told me that if I put it on the table and gave it some oats and said, "Hen, hen, lay your eggs," I would get a great surprise.'

'Let's do it now and see what happens,' said the farmer's wife.

'All right,' said Jack and he went out and got the hen and put her on the table.

The farmer's wife gave her some oats and Jack said: 'Hen, hen, lay your eggs.'

The hen picked at the oats and at the same time she began to lay golden eggs as fast as one could count them. By the time she had finished the oats she had laid about twenty.

The people of the house were delighted and so was Jack. They gave him a lovely bed in the best room and made a nest for the hen beside the bed.

Next morning he set out for home, taking with him the hen and a big griddle cake which the woman of the house had made for him.

His mother was filled with joy to see her son again. After he had told her about his travels, he showed her what he said was the most wonderful hen in Eirinn.

'She looks just like any other hen,' said his mother.

'Put some oats on the table and you'll soon see, Mother,' he said.

She did as he told her and then he put the hen on the table beside the oats and said, 'Hen, hen, lay your eggs.' But the hen went on picking and not an egg did she lay.

'Oh, my poor foolish boy!' said the mother. 'You had no sense when you left home and you have less now.'

'I have been cheated, Mother,' said Jack, 'but I will try my fortune again.' And then he told her about the hen that laid the golden eggs.

'That farmer and his family cheated you indeed,' said his mother. 'Tomorrow morning go off to the old woman again and tell her what has happened.'

He went off again and arrived at the farmer's house. He told them that the hen would not lay any golden eggs for him. They laughed and pretended they had never seen the hen that laid the golden eggs and that Jack had only dreamed all that nonsense. Poor Jack did not know what to think, and when he returned to the old woman he told her all that had happened.

'You were foolish, Jack,' she said, 'to try to find out what the hen could do till you went home. The hen you brought to your mother was not the one I gave you.'

'I wonder,' said Jack, 'would the kind people who gave me such a welcome do such a mean thing as to steal the hen?'

'You can't help it now. Go back to your work of minding the animals,' said the old woman.

The cows and all the other animals were glad to have Jack back, for he was very kind to them. After a week, the old woman told him to go home again to see his mother.

'Here is a tablecloth,' she said, 'but do not open it till you reach your own home. Then spread it on the table and say, "Tablecloth, do your duty."'

Jack set out again the next day and soon he came to the farmer's house. He kept the tablecloth round his body so that the people of the house would not see it. They made jokes about what they called his dream and asked him what wages he had got this time.

Jack would not tell them, but at last one of the children peeped under his coat and saw the cloth.

They teased him and laughed at him so much that in the end he spread the cloth on the table and, forgetting the old woman's warning, said:

'Tablecloth, do your duty.'

In a moment it was covered with golden plates, jugs, tumblers, knives and forks. The dishes contained delicious foods and the jugs and tumblers were filled with the richest wine. Everyone had a most delightful meal and when it was over Jack gave all the golden utensils to the woman of the house.

That night he was given the same fine bed as he had slept in on the other night, and the farmer's wife put the tablecloth under his pillow.

Next morning he got up early and taking the tablecloth from under his pillow, he set out for home. When he got there, he took out the tablecloth and showed it to his mother. However, when he put the cloth on the table he was very disappointed to find that neither golden vessels nor fine food appeared. His mother shook her head at him for being so foolish, but he determined to go again to the house under the furze bush.

On his way back he stayed with the farmer's family. They laughed at him when he spoke of the tablecloth.

'It was another dream you had, Jack,' said they, 'a dream like the one you had about the hen.'

When Jack came to the old woman's house and

told her all that had happened, she told him she had only one gift left.

'Take this stick,' she said, 'and whenever you say, "Stick, do your duty," you will see something that will surprise you, but be careful, for this is the last present I will give you.'

Jack thanked her and set out for home once more.

On his way home he stayed at the farmer's house again. Jack did not hide his gift this time and the people of the house talked a good deal about it.

At last Jack said, 'Well, as I showed you what the hen could do and what the tablecloth could do, or, as you say, what I dreamed they could do, I will show you what the stick can do, but first let me warn you it may all be a dream.'

'I think it is,' said the farmer's wife with a smile.

'Now,' said he, 'stick, do your duty.'

On the moment the stick flew from one to another of the whole household, whacking and beating every member, until there were shouts of pain and panic from every side. It moved like lightning, and just as a person would be rising from a blow, back came the stick to give him another thrashing.

'Oh, Jack!' cried the woman of the house. 'Stop the stick and we will give you back your hen.'

'But you said, my good woman, that the hen was only a dream,' said Jack.

'Oh, here she is for you, Jack, and stop the stick,'

she begged. She opened a door and there sat Jack's hen.

'Stick, stick, will that do?' asked Jack, but the stick went on beating harder than ever.

'Oh, Jack!' cried the woman, 'here is your table-cloth.' Opening a drawer, she took out the cloth and gave it to him.

'Stick, stick, stop now,' said Jack. The stick flew back to Jack's hand, but the farmer and his family continued moaning with pain for a long time as they rubbed their aching limbs.

Jack would not stay a moment longer among such deceitful people. He slept in a shed and reached home in the evening. His mother's joy knew no bounds when she saw the wonderful hen and the magic cloth.

She and Jack lived very happily together, and because of the magic gifts, they never saw a poor day again. However, they spent their money wisely and were very good to the poor.

One day they drove in a carriage to the place where the old fairy woman had lived. The furze and the rock were there, but the house had disappeared. There was no trace of cows or sheep or the other animals. All was silent and still, and Jack never saw his kind old friend again.

Conn's Three Friends

One day some wicked boys were ill-treating a mouse which they had caught. A kind-hearted young man named Conn happened to pass by. 'Oh! boys,' said he, 'if you stop teasing that mouse, I'll give you six-pence.' So the boys took the money, ran off, and the mouse was set free.

Conn went along the road and what should he meet but a group of cruel youngsters beating a weasel. 'Oh! let that animal go,' said Conn, handing them a shilling.

Some time after this he came upon some young men who were tormenting a poor donkey, so he gave them half-a-crown to set the donkey free.

'Now,' said Neddy the donkey, 'you have been a good friend to me and I would like to be a faithful servant to you. Get up on my back and I will carry you, for the day is hot and I am sure you must be tired.'

After they had journeyed on for a time, Conn got down off the donkey's back and stretched himself under a shady tree. Very soon he fell into a deep sleep. He slept for some time, but was awakened suddenly by a fierce-looking man who, with his two servants, was standing beside him.

'What do you mean,' said the man, 'by letting your donkey stray into my fine meadow?'

'I did not know he was in the meadow and I beg your pardon for any damage he has done.'

'Beg my pardon, did you say? I'll show you the pardon you'll get. Bring out the big trunk from the kitchen,' said the man to his servants.

Poor Conn was forced into the trunk. The trunk was then tied with a hempen rope and thrown into the river.

The three men went away and there was the poor donkey, standing on the river bank, braying as loud as he could. Up came the mouse and the weasel. They asked him what was the matter. He told them that the kind man who had saved him from the cruelty of the idle youths had been put into the big trunk which they saw floating down the river.

'Oh,' said the weasel, 'that must be the same man that saved me.'

'And me, too,' said the mouse.

'Had he a coat with a brown patch on the sleeve?' asked the weasel.

'He had,' said the donkey.

'That's the man,' said the mouse. 'We must try to save him.'

The weasel mounted on the donkey's back, the mouse got into his ear and the donkey plunged into the river. They had not gone very far when they saw the trunk standing in the water where it had been stopped by some rushes. It was close to the edge of a little island. They crossed the island and before long the weasel and the mouse had gnawed the rope and Conn jumped out of the trunk.

As the four were standing by the river, the weasel saw a beautifully coloured egg lying in the water close to the edge. He picked it up with his mouth and gave it to Conn.

Conn turned it round in his hand and, as he did so, he happened to say: 'Oh, how I would love to have a fine castle where we could all live together!'

Hardly had he uttered these words than he and his friends were transported to a magnificent castle, surrounded with beautiful grounds. There was no owner or landlord to be seen anywhere. Conn and his friends took up their abode in the castle. It was beautifully furnished and they found a lot of money in a cupboard in one of the rooms.

Conn and his friends were very happy until one

day when he was standing at the door of the castle three merchants with their goods came by.

'What is the meaning of this?' asked one. 'Last time we passed by this place there was no castle here.'

'No,' said another, 'nor park nor lands.'

'You speak the truth,' said Conn, 'but come in and rest for the night.'

The merchants gladly accepted this invitation and when they were all enjoying a good dinner, poor, simple Conn told them the story of the egg. The wily merchants watched their opportunity and slipped a powder into Conn's tumbler and soon the poor fellow was sound asleep. When he awoke he found himself back on the island with the donkey, the weasel and the mouse. They were very sad. The weasel thought for a while and then asked Conn if he remembered the name and address of the merchants. Fortunately he did remember. The weasel got on the donkey's back and the mouse got into his ear and they all went off to find their enemies.

They reached the house of the principal merchant and the mouse went in. He came back and told his friends that the egg was in a press in the merchant's room but that it was guarded by two cats who were chained to the press.

When night came the weasel told the mouse to go to the merchant's bed and keep sucking his hair as long as he could.

Next morning when the merchant found the state in which the mouse had left his hair he let loose the two cats and told them that when he went to sleep that night they were to sit near his pillow till morning.

That night the weasel and the mouse gnawed a hole in the door. When the cats fell asleep the mouse went in and pushed the egg through the hole. Then they all started off, the mouse in the donkey's ear, the weasel on his back and the egg in the weasel's mouth.

When they were swimming across the river the donkey began to bray. He thought he was a great fellow. He wanted his friends to praise him but the mouse was asleep in his ear and the weasel had the egg in his mouth.

'If you don't praise and thank me,' said the donkey, 'I'll shake you off.'

The weasel was frightened.

'Please don't,' he said, and with that down fell the egg in the water. The donkey was sorry and very much ashamed, but the clever weasel thought of a plan to recover the egg. He looked down at the frogs and fishes in the water and he told them a big army was coming to take them out and eat them. He said the only way they could save themselves was to gather up all the stones from the bottom of the water and give them to him and his companions. They would use the stones to build a wall to keep the army away. The fishes and frogs began bringing up the stones and at last one big frog brought up the egg. The weasel then told the fishes they were safe now as the army had run away when they had seen the wall.

Conn soon had his castle back again and he and his three friends were very happy together. After a time he married a beautiful girl and she, too, became the friend and companion of the mouse, the weasel and good old Neddy, the donkey.

The Disguised Princess

Princess Eithne lived in a fine palace with her mother, Queen Rose, and her stepfather, King Conal. Eithne disliked her stepfather very much because he was a harsh and cruel man.

Queen Rose died and the princess was very lonely after her. One day King Conal sent a message to Princess Eithne to come at once to the throne room. The princess wondered what her stepfather could want with her, but she did as he asked.

When she reached the throne room, she was surprised to find a tall, dark stranger with King Conal, and when the stranger turned to face her, she saw that he had a very ugly, wicked face.

'This is Prince Igon, who is going to marry you,' said King Conal. 'He is a great friend of mine, so you must do as I say.'

The poor girl was very unhappy. She had a beautiful mare that she thought was the creature in all the world that loved her best, so she told this mare her sad story.

The mare was really a fairy in disguise and she was a sort of guardian to this princess. To her surprise, the mare spoke to Eithne and told her, 'Don't be uneasy. I will help you. Tell your stepfather that you will not marry till you get a dress made of silk and silver thread and that the dress must fit into a walnut shell. I will delay the workers so that he will be kept a long time waiting.'

Princess Eithne did as her friend, the mare, told her and asked King Conal for a dress made of silk and silver thread that would fit into a walnut shell.

He didn't like the marriage to be delayed, but he yielded to her wishes and ordered the court dress-makers to make it as quickly as they could. They worked hard at their sewing, but something seemed to delay them every day, and so the dress wasn't ready for many months. When the dress was finished, the king thought that Princess Eithne would marry Prince Igon, but on the mare's advice she told him she wanted another dress — this time one made of silk and gold thread — and that it, too, must fit into a walnut shell.

Again the mare worked her magic and the making

of the dress was very slow, but it was finished at last.

'Surely,' said King Conal, 'you will marry Igon now.'

'I will not marry,' said Princess Eithne, 'till I get a dress of silk thread covered with pearls and diamonds. It, too, must fit into a walnut shell.'

King Conal was disappointed and angry but he ordered the dress for her. 'This is the last one you will get,' he said.

After a long delay the dress was ready, but at the same time the mare gave Eithne a dress of cat-skins. The princess put this on and put the three walnuts in her pocket. On the advice of the mare she stained her face and hands with a brown colour and in this disguise she mounted the mare and before daybreak they were miles away from the palace.

They reached a wood and Eithne dismounted. She sat down under a shady tree and was soon in a sound sleep. Suddenly she was awakened by the barking and yelping of dogs. They looked very fierce when they saw the cat-skins, but a hunter came up and called them to him. The hunter was none other than King Brian, who was famous throughout the land for his valour and kindness. He thought the princess was a very pretty girl, but wondered at her strange colour and the extraordinary dress she wore. When he found that she was alone and friendless, he brought her to his palace and gave orders that she should be employed in the kitchen.

The other servants laughed at Eithne's strange dress and called her 'Cat-skins'. She was given a very, very small bedroom, far away from the other apartments.

To the great surprise and annoyance of the household, King Brian asked that Cat-skins should be his own personal attendant. When she came into his presence he asked her many questions, but though he knew from her voice and manner that she was of noble birth, he could get very little information from her.

One night King Brian attended a great ball in a nearby castle. That same night, the princess, having washed the stain from her face and hands, went to bed early. She could not sleep, however, and rose and went out in the cool air. What should she see but the mare under a tree. The mare told her to open the first walnut shell.

'Now,' said the mare, 'hold the dress over your head and put it on.'

When Eithne was clothed in the beautiful silk and silver dress, the mare, who wore fine harness, told her to mount on her back. Off they galloped and soon they arrived at the castle where the ball was being held.

Everyone was amazed when the beautifully dressed girl entered. King Brian came forward to meet her and spent the rest of the night by her side.

He was very sorry when she said she must go home and wished that she would allow his servants to attend her on the way. She told him she preferred to go alone and that the mare was waiting for her. He helped her into the saddle and she was off like a flash.

Next morning Princess Eithne put on her cat-skin dress and stained her hands and face.

The king sent for her. While she was working he looked at her and thought that but for the colour of her skin, she looked very like the beautiful lady who had come to the ball. He questioned her about her home and people, but her answers told him very little.

In a short time there was another great ball. King Brian went to it and when he had gone, Eithne put on her silk and gold dress and, mounting her friend the mare, she followed him there. She looked even more beautiful than she had at the first ball and the king fell more deeply in love with her. When she was leaving he again begged to be allowed to accompany her, but Eithne told him that she preferred to go alone. However, she promised him that she would come to the next ball, which was to be held a week later.

In the morning, when she was sewing a button on the king's cuff, he noticed how small and well-shaped was her hand, but when he questioned her she finished her work quickly and hurried away.

At the third ball, Princess Eithne was dazzlingly

beautiful in her dress of silk with the pearls and diamonds. King Brian wished to accompany her to her home and was very sad when she again said that she must go alone.

'However,' the princess said, 'if you know me next time you see me, we shall never part again.'

When she was seated on the mare, King Brian managed to slip a very small ring on her finger without her noticing it.

Next morning he sent for her. He told her that he wished to ask her opinion about certain clothes, as he was going to be married. Eithne said that a poor girl like her could not advise him and that he had better consult the beautiful lady about whom all the servants were talking.

'I suppose she will be your bride,' she said.

'It is just as probable that you will be my bride,' said King Brian.

'I your bride!' Eithne exclaimed.

'Yes, because you and the beautiful lady are one. That ring on your finger tells me so. You promised we would part no more if I knew you the next time we met. I claim you now as my bride.'

Princess Eithne went out hurriedly and returned in a short time. She had washed off the brown stain and put on her dress of silk and jewels.

'Now,' she said when she came back, 'I'm fit to be your bride.'

The marriage took place almost immediately and one of the principal guests was the fairy who had disguised herself as the mare and who now appeared as a beautiful woman.

The wedding feast lasted for three days and three nights and King Brian and his bride lived happily ever after.

The Magic Bracelet

There's an old Irish saying which tells us that 'However long the day is, night comes at last.'

King Felimy and Queen Cliodhna lived very happily together in their castle by the banks of Lough Dubh. They had one little daughter, Princess Maeveen, who was the light of their eyes.

The queen and her daughter spent every morning working together. In summer they would gather flowers in the garden and arrange them in vases, or they would feed Mikeleen the canary, or help the cook to make jam. In the winter they would sit by the fire and do fine embroidery or make lace.

One cold winter's morning when Princess Maeveen and her mother were sitting by the fire, the queen suddenly became very pale and fell on the floor in a dead faint. The princess rushed out to get some water and in a few minutes the ladies-in-waiting had carried their mistress to her room. The court doctors came and did all they could to cure Queen Cliodhna, but in a few days they told King Felimy that they could do no more.

The oldest and wisest of the doctors drew the king aside and said: 'We have used all our wisdom and knowledge and yet we cannot heal your wife. In a few days she will die.'

Now Queen Cliodhna knew that she was very ill and that she might soon die, so she called Princess Maeveen to her bedside.

'Little daughter,' she said, 'take this key and open the golden box which stands on the table by the window.' Maeveen did as she was told.

'Lift out that bracelet,' said the queen, 'and bring it to me.'

The princess lifted out a bracelet made of hair silk and golden threads and brought it to her mother.

Queen Cliodhna fastened it on her daughter's left arm, just above the elbow, and said, 'This bracelet was given to me by a good fairy shortly after your birth. You must always wear it, for while you do, no evil can harm you. Guard it carefully because if any other woman should take it from you and wear it, she will have complete power over you.'

A few days later Queen Cliodhna died and everybody mourned her death.

There was a woman at King Felimy's court called Siobhaun Rua who had been a lady-in-waiting to the dead queen.

When her mistress died, she and her daughter Pampoge remained at the court to look after Princess Maeveen. Now Pampoge was a very ugly, bad-tempered girl, and she was very jealous of the princess, who was beautiful and kind. However, her mother, Siobhaun Rua, was very good to the little princess and Maeveen was very fond of her.

Noticing this and thinking that he would not be so lonely if he married again, King Felimy asked Siobhaun Rua to be his wife. She consented and they were married soon afterward.

For a while everybody at the court was very happy. However, a year had not gone by before the new queen and her daughter showed themselves in their true colours. When her father was not about, they treated Princess Maeveen very badly. They refused to give her food, they pulled her hair, they made her work in the kitchen and they warned her that if she told her father about it, they would beat her.

The poor princess was lonely and unhappy, for she was afraid of the wicked Siobhaun Rua. There was nobody she could tell her sad story to except Faireen, her little pet dog, and often she used to sit with Faireen on her knee, telling him again and again how cruel Siobhaun and Pampoge were and crying over it.

One day a messenger rode into the castle yard and asked to see the king. When he was brought to King Felimy, he explained that he had been sent by Prince Conall, his master, who begged permission to come to visit Princess Maeveen.

King Felimy had often heard of Prince Conall, for he was well known through the length and breadth of Ireland for his courage, his deeds of valour and daring, and for his kindness and courtesy.

He would gladly have this brave young prince marry his daughter, so he told the messenger that Prince Conall would be welcome at his castle.

The messenger thanked the king and rode away as fast as his horse would carry him.

Five days later Prince Conall and his servants arrived at the palace.

When Princess Maeveen and the handsome prince met, they fell deeply in love with each other, and soon afterward Prince Conall asked the king for his daughter's hand in marriage. King Felimy gladly consented and there was great rejoicing at the court. But Siobhaun Rua and her daughter were jealous and angry because they envied the good fortune of the princess.

The next day Prince Conall left the castle and went home to prepare for his wedding. Before he went, he made the princess promise that she would follow him in ten days' time, so that they could be married at his own castle. Princess Maeveen gladly gave him her promise and he rode away.

The princess spent the next ten days in great excitement, preparing for her wedding, but when the time came for her to go, she was sad at leaving her beloved father.

'Bring Pampoge with you, Maeveen,' said King Felimy. 'She will help you to forget your loneliness.'

This suited Siobhaun Rua and Pampoge very well, for they were planning to harm Princess Maeveen if they could. However, no harm could befall her as long as she wore her magic bracelet, so first of all they would have to try to take it from her.

'Leave that to me, Mother,' Pampoge said. 'I'll get it from her, all right.'

'You will, Daughter,' said Siobhaun Rua with a wicked smile. 'And maybe you'd marry Prince Conall yourself.'

'Maybe I would,' said Pampoge.

Princess Maeveen set out with Pampoge and many attendants for the palace where Prince Conall lived. It was a long journey, and riding along in the hot sunshine made them both very tired and very thirsty. On the second day of their journey, the heat seemed to be worse than ever, so when the princess saw a lake glittering in the valley below them, she said to Pampoge, 'Let's go down and bathe in the lake. It will cool us.'

Pampoge agreed and they dismounted. The princess told the servants they could rest in the shelter of the trees while she and her stepsister bathed in the lake.

Princess Maeveen and Pampoge ran down the hillside to the shore of the lake. The water was cool and pleasant and Maeveen swam around and around and enjoyed herself very much. Pampoge didn't stay in very long but soon hopped out and dressed. When the princess grew tired of bathing, she swam to the spot at the water's edge where she had left her clothes. To her dismay, she saw that they weren't there! Then she noticed that Pampoge was perched on the branch of a nearby tree with an evil smile on her face.

'Ha! Ha! Ha!' she laughed. 'Come and climb for your clothes, proud princess!'

Princess Maeveen at first thought that Pampoge was joking, but when she saw that this was not so she begged her to return her clothes.

'You can have them if you give me that bracelet you're wearing,' said Pampoge.

'Here you are,' said Maeveen, forgetting her mother's warning and handing the bracelet to Pampoge.

Pampoge took the bracelet and put it on her left arm just above the elbow. 'Now, my fine Maeveen,' she said with a bitter laugh, 'I have you in my power.' It was then that Princess Maeveen remembered her mother's words about the magic bracelet and she knew that she was indeed in Pampoge's power.

'I will cast a spell on you,' said Pampoge. 'From now on you will look like me and I will look like you. Nobody will believe that you are really Princess Maeveen!'

Then she ordered Maeveen to dress in her clothes while she dressed in Maeveen's.

'Look at me!' said the bold Pampoge. 'Who could say that I am not Princess Maeveen?'

And looking at her, Maeveen knew that what she said was true. Running down to the water's edge, she looked at her own reflection there and, to her horror, she saw not her own pretty face and golden hair, but the ugly, bad-tempered face and straggling hair of Pampoge.

'If you ever tell a human being about what happened today, I'll turn you into a toad!' Pampoge warned Maeveen.

'Now, come on and let us finish our journey; I cannot wait to see my dear Prince Conall.'

They climbed back to the road where the attendants waited for them, and, of course, everyone took Pampoge for the real princess.

When they arrived at the prince's castle, he too thought that Pampoge was his beloved Maeveen. He was surprised and hurt when she was rude and nasty to him, for during his visit to King Felimy's castle she was never like that. As the days passed, he grew weary of her stupid conversation and bad temper, and he wished that he had not promised to marry her.

While Pampoge was being entertained at the castle as Princess Maeveen, the real princess was working in the kitchen as a scullery maid. She was kind and gentle, even though she looked ugly, and everyone was very fond of her. But the poor girl was very unhappy and the only thing that consoled her was little Faireen, her dog. Faireen used to walk with her through the fields and the princess would tell him all her troubles. The little dog would wag his tail and lick her hands to show her how sorry he was.

One day when Princess Maeveen was feeling very sad she sat in a little summer-house which was hidden behind a laburnum tree at the end of the garden.

Little Faireen followed her there, and taking her pet in her arms the princess told him of Pampoge's wickedness.

'Oh, my poor little friend, I can tell you what I must never tell any human being. My cruel stepsister Pampoge stole from me my magic bracelet and fastened it on her own left arm. This bracelet kept me from harm but now I'm in her power. She cast a spell on me so that I look like her and she has taken my place as princess. Everybody, even Prince Conall, thinks that she is really Princess Maeveen. Oh, I'm so unhappy, Faireen! What can I do?' she sighed.

Faireen wagged his little tail and licked Maeveen's hand to show how sorry he was, but he could do nothing to help her.

Now one of the woodchoppers chanced to be passing the summer-house just then and he heard what Maeveen was saying to Faireen. 'I must tell my master what I have heard,' he said to himself. 'If it is true, he will surely give me a reward.' So he hurried off to the courtyard where Prince Conall was preparing to go hunting.

The prince listened to his story and then he warned the woodchopper not to breathe a word of it to anyone else. He also promised him a rich reward for his kindness in helping to free the poor princess.

Instead of going hunting, Prince Conall went to his father, the king, and told him the story.

'Bring the princess here,' said the king to one of his courtiers, and in a few moments the false princess came in.

'Do you wear a bracelet on your left arm?' the king asked. Pampoge knew that it was useless to deny that she did, and she said that she had always worn the bracelet, ever since she was a child.

'Please show it to me,' said the king. She pushed up the sleeve of her dress and showed him the bracelet.

'Take it off,' he said. 'I want to examine it.'

Now Pampoge did not know how to open the

bracelet, for it had a magic clasp on it. 'I can't,' she said.

'I know somebody who can ... and here she is,' said Prince Conall, bringing Maeveen into the room.

Pampoge flew into a raging temper when she saw the real princess. 'You broke your promise!' she shouted. 'I'll turn you into a toad for this!' But the prince was too quick for her, and catching her by the arm so that she could not move, he told Maeveen to unclasp the bracelet.

At her touch the bracelet opened and Maeveen slipped it onto her own left arm. Instantly a change came over the two girls — Princess Maeveen became her beautiful self once more and Pampoge became as ugly as she had ever been.

Prince Conall was overjoyed to find his real bride again and in a few days he and Princess Maeveen were married.

The woodchopper was made the prince's chief huntsman, and little Faireen was given a nice, new kennel to live in and a fresh, juicy bone every day. As for the wicked Pampoge — she was banished to the dark wood of Egin and was never seen or heard of again.

The wedding feast of Prince Conall and Princess Maeveen lasted three days and three nights, and the last night was better than the first.

The Kettle's Song

Once upon a time there was a little lame girl named Deirdre, who lived in a poor cabin near the shores of Lough Mask in County Mayo. She could not remember her mother because she had died when Deirdre was very young. Her father married again. His second wife had been a widow and she had a daughter named Gobnet. Deirdre's father died shortly after his second marriage. She was now very unhappy, for both her stepmother and her stepsister hated her. They were a cruel, hardhearted pair. Deirdre was very helpless. She could not walk. Every morning her stepmother and Gobnet lifted her from her bed, not too gently indeed, and carried her to a chair beside the fire. They never spoke kindly to her.

'Be sure to keep the fire burning,' the stepmother would say, as she placed a large basket of turf near Deirdre before going out to work on the little farm.

'And mind you have the kettle nearly boiling when we come in,' would be the order from the daughter.

As mealtime came on, Deirdre would move the kettle nearer the fire. She came to regard the kettle as a sort of companion. It had been in the house longer than she could remember, for it had belonged to her mother. When it began to sing she fancied its song had a message of hope and joy for her.

She dared not talk about the kettle to her step-mother, nor to Gobnet, but she had one friend who was very kind to her in the midst of all her loneliness and sorrow. A strange friend he was indeed. He lived with his mother in a small house about half a mile away and was known as Tim the *amadán* [fool]. He was a huge fellow, seven feet high, with shaggy dark hair, bushy eyebrows and a long black beard. Poor Tim had little sense; but he was very kind to Deirdre and together they often listened to the kettle's song. In spring and summer he would come into the little kitchen with great bunches of wild flowers. Deirdre loved specially the forget-me-nots which Tim told her grew near the lovely lake. In the blackberry season the two friends had great feasts. The stepmother hated Tim. He took care not to go near the house when she was at home.

Years went by till Deirdre was a grown girl. She had a beautiful face and her lovely dark hair was long and glossy, but she was still unable to move from her chair without help.

One autumn night the stepmother and her daughter were enjoying themselves listening to stories in a neighbour's house. Deirdre was sitting alone. She moved the kettle nearer the fire and soon the steam began to come from the spout. As she watched, the steam changed into different colours and formed a lovely rainbow in the little kitchen. More wonderful still, Deirdre saw sitting at the foot of the rainbow a tiny woman. The woman began to sing in a sweet little voice:

> 'At the hazel near the mill,
> While the sleeping world is still,
> I wait at night,
> When the moon is bright,
> To comfort every ill.'

The rainbow disappeared and the little woman with it, as Deirdre heard her stepmother and Gobnet returning.

In the morning when Deirdre was alone she heard the heavy tread of Tim's feet as he came towards the door.

'Hah! hah! hah! and how are you today, Deirdre?'

Poor Tim was always laughing.

'Oh, Tim!' exclaimed Deirdre. 'I am delighted to see you for I have something wonderful to tell you.'

'Hah! hah! hah!' was Tim's only reply.

'Oh, stop laughing for a minute, Tim, till I tell you what happened here in the kitchen last night.'

'Did the kettle sing a new song?' asked Tim.

'Yes,' answered Deirdre, 'and I have heard another wonderful song, too.'

Then she told him all about the rainbow and the little woman.

'Oh, Tim, if only I could go to the hazel tree, perhaps I would be made well and strong, but I can never leave this house.'

'Poor Deirdre,' said Tim. Then he began to laugh and to hug himself with glee. 'Listen,' he said, 'I will go to the tree. The moon is full just now and I will start off tonight. Perhaps I will be able to get a cure for you.'

'Oh, how good you are, Tim! But mind you don't tell anyone you are going.'

'No one will hear anything from me; but your ugly stepmother and her ugly daughter will be coming home soon now, so I will not stay any longer. Good night, Deirdre.'

'Good night, Tim, and thank you very much.'

That night Deirdre was sitting alone in the kitchen. The kettle began to sing. As the song continued these words reached her ears:

'While here you stay,
At close of day,
A friend both kind and true
Seeks help and health,
And peace and wealth,
To cheer and comfort you.'

At the same time Tim had set out for the hazel tree. He had to walk a long distance to reach it. As he came near the tree, he saw a tiny little woman standing near it. He knew this was the woman Deirdre had seen in the kitchen. She looked so small and Tim was so big that he burst out laughing. The woman laughed with him.

'Who are you?' she asked.

'I am Tim, the fool.'

'I don't think you are much of a fool but tell me why you have come here.'

'Deirdre told me about the song you sang last night and I came here to try to find something to make her well and strong.'

'Well, Tim, I would like to cure her for her mother was very kind to us fairies. She never took grass from the moat, nor flowers from the fairy thorn, and she used to leave a basin of clean water near the fire at night so that the fairies could take a drink when they visited her house on their midnight travels.'

'Deirdre herself is very good,' said Tim.

'I know that, and I will try to make her strong, but do you not want anything for yourself, Tim?'

'No, indeed, I will be quite satisfied if Deirdre is cured.'

'All right, but later on I will give a special gift in the form of hidden treasure to you yourself because you are so unselfish and so good to other people.'

'Hah! hah! hah!' laughed Tim.

'Did you ever hear, Tim, that if you were able to find the foot of a rainbow you would see there a crock of gold?'

'Indeed I did, and many an hour I spent chasing rainbows.'

'Perhaps,' said the little woman, 'you are not the only one who has lost time in that way. Now,' she continued, 'Deirdre has told you she saw me sitting at the foot of the rainbow in her home last night. Perhaps I could have found the crock of gold there if I wished to look for it.'

'Indeed,' said Tim, 'I hope you did for you deserve a reward for your kindness.'

'We won't talk more of the gold now but I will tell you what to do if you wish to cure Deirdre. You see that narrow little lane there.'

'Yes,' said Tim, 'but I never went near it because the fairies have their home at the end of that lane.'

'You must go to the end of it now,' said the woman, 'and there you will find a fairy mound surrounded by trees. In circles round the mound are three rows of stones. Step over the first one, then over the second but do not pass the third. In the centre of the third row is a sloe bush. These sloes have wonderful healing power. They can cure any disease. If Deirdre eats one of them, she will at once become well and strong.'

'But,' said Tim, 'won't the fairies harm me if I go near their fort?'

'They will, if they know you are among them, but listen to me and I will tell you what to do. Crowds of fairies in the form of little dwarfs hide behind the trees. Each has a poisoned arrow. If any mortal attempts to approach the fort, they will shoot him.'

'Well, then, won't they shoot me?' asked Tim.

'No, not if you follow my instructions. You must be daring and brave if you wish to save Deirdre. She will die soon if she does not get the magic sloe.'

'Oh!' exclaimed Tim. 'What would I do if Deirdre died?'

'She will not die but will get well and strong, if you do as I tell you. You see those nuts on the tree.'

'Yes,' said Tim. 'The moon is so bright that I can see even the smallest of them.'

'Pull three nuts from the tree, a large one, a medium-sized one and a small one.'

Tim pulled the nuts.

'Now,' said the woman, 'when you come to the entrance of the lane eat the small nut. Immediately you will become as tiny as the smallest dwarf. Slip in among the fairies. They will think you are one of themselves for the nut has power to change your clothes and whole appearance. The Queen and her fairies will be dancing at the far side of the mound. Go quickly to the bush. Gather a sloe and hurry back.'

'But how will I get out of the fort?'

'The dwarfs sometimes go outside the circle to see if any mortal is near. They will not notice that you have gone. Hurry to the far end of the lane. Then eat the large nut. Immediately, you will resume your own shape and appearance.'

'And what shall I do with the third nut?'

'Keep it and eat it when Deirdre is cured but you must not speak a word to her until you have eaten the nut. Go to her house tomorrow night when the moon is high in the sky.

> 'Now haste and go,
> To find the sloe,
> And then return again,
> To bring relief
> From woe and grief,
> From sickness and from pain.'

Tim thanked the woman and hurried towards the lane. At the entrance he ate the small nut and at once he became a little dwarf with a bow and arrow in his hand. He ran lightly down the lane and slipped quietly in among the trees. As he looked towards the mound he saw a number of dwarfs there. He climbed over the first stone circle, then over the second and reached over the third to gather the sloe. He hurried back and slipped out again from among the trees. He ran like lightning up the lane. When he reached the end he ate the large nut and was his big, strong self again. There was no sign of the little woman when he reached the hazel tree. He hurried home and put the sloe and the hazel nut safely in a cupboard.

Next morning Deirdre was so ill that she could not be taken from her bed. Neither her stepmother nor Gobnet took any care of her. When night came on, they both went out to enjoy a chat and storytelling at a house some distance away. The moon began to shine through the window of the little room where she lay. She feared she would not live to see its light when it rose the next night. She wondered why Tim had not called that day and felt very sad and lonely. Later on the stepmother and Gobnet returned home. The kettle was put on the fire. It began to sing.

'I will listen to its song for the last time,' thought poor Deirdre.

These words seemed woven into the tune:

> 'Be of good cheer,
> For help is near,
> Fear not death nor grief,

Nor pain nor woe,
For the fairy sloe
Brings comfort and relief.'

Suddenly there was a loud knocking at the kitchen door. The stepmother, who was in the act of lifting the kettle from the fire, turned and laid it down on one of the flags on the kitchen floor.

'Hah! hah! hah! let me in,' came in a loud voice from outside.

'That is Tim the fool,' said Gobnet.

'Don't let him in,' said the stepmother in a loud voice.

Tim heard her and shouted through the door, 'If you don't let me in, I'll climb up on the house and make a hole in the roof and come in whether you like it or not.'

'Well, we won't let you in,' said both women together.

Then they heard sounds of stepping and climbing and in a few moments Tim's long legs descended through the thatch. The mother and daughter rushed from the house and did not return till the next day.

Tim went quietly into the little room where Deirdre lay. She was almost dying. He lifted her head gently and placed the sloe in her mouth. In a moment she rose from the bed completely cured. Not only was she strong and well but she was dressed in a robe of rich silk and looked very beautiful.

'Oh, dear Tim!' she cried. 'How can I thank you, and how has all this happened?'

To her surprise, Tim did not utter a word. She watched him in wonder as he took the hazel nut from his pocket and put it in his mouth. Then, to her amazement, she saw standing before her not a huge, awkward man but a handsome youth dressed in fine clothes.

At last Tim spoke. He told her all about the little woman, the dwarfs, the nuts and the sloe.

'You can no longer stay in this house,' he said. 'Come and you and I will get married and live with my mother in our little house till we can find a better one.'

They went together into the kitchen and saw the kettle in the middle of the floor.

'I would like to take the kettle with me,' said Deirdre. 'It belonged to my mother and all our happiness has come through it.'

Tim lifted the kettle. As he did so the flagstone on which it had rested came away with it and fell with a crash on the floor, and there in a hole under where the flagstone had been was a huge crock of gold.

'Oh,' said Tim, 'this is the gold the little woman spoke of. She said she could have found it at the foot of the rainbow.'

'It was just at the spot where the flagstone was that I saw the woman sitting at the foot of the rainbow,' cried Deirdre.

'And she promised me a gift in the form of hidden treasure, so now I can make you a great lady,' said Tim. 'You must carry the kettle, Deirdre,' he added, 'for I will require all my strength to carry this big crock.'

Joyfully they went from the place where Deirdre had suffered so much and soon they were living in a beautiful house. They had costly furniture and many valuable possessions but amongst them all none was so much prized and treasured as the old kettle.

The Emerald Ring

O nce upon a time there lived in Munster a king named Mahon with his queen, Una. They had a beautiful daughter named Emer. Suitors came from all parts of Eirinn and even from beyond the sea to seek her hand in marriage. Emer, however, had made her own choice.

'I will marry no one but Flan, the young King of Connacht,' she said.

'In my opinion,' declared King Mahon, 'you could not find a better husband and I am sure that is your mother's opinion, too.'

'Indeed it is,' said the queen.

The wedding preparations began at once.

One day the queen called her daughter to her and said:

'This emerald ring which I constantly wear was given to me by my mother a short time before my marriage. I shall now give it to you as a wedding gift.'

'Oh, thank you, Mother!' said Emer. 'I have always liked that ring and I think it is very beautiful.'

'It is beautiful,' replied the queen, 'but it is valuable for another reason as well as for its beauty. It has the power to protect you from harm. If your life is ever threatened by an enemy, the emerald will become black as night to warn you that danger is near.'

'I do not think I have any enemy, Mother, but I shall wear the ring night and day and shall treasure it beyond all my gifts.'

Now there was a princess in Connacht named Maeve who wished to marry King Flan. When she found that a wedding was arranged between him and Emer, she became nearly mad with jealousy. She set out at once for Munster. Here she lived in a little hut hidden among a clump of bushes. A well nearby supplied her with water and she had brought provisions with her when she was leaving home. The hut was not far from King Mahon's castle. She hoped to find out all about the wedding preparations and to discover some way of preventing the marriage.

Unfortunately, anyone who is determined to commit an evil deed will always find means to do it.

One day Maeve wandered far away from all human habitation until she came to a forest. As she went farther in among the trees, she could hardly see the way but the darkness suited her gloomy and wicked thoughts. All at once she heard a harsh, grating laugh. The sound seemed to come from the top of one of the trees. She looked up. There, sitting on one of the highest branches, was a hideously ugly old hag with a lantern in her hand. She wore a long black cloak with a hood. From out of the hood her grey hair streamed almost into her eyes. Turning the light of the lantern on Maeve's upturned face, she said: 'You look unhappy, fair stranger. What is your trouble?'

'I am unhappy,' said Maeve, 'and I cannot find anyone to help me to do as I wish.'

'What is it that you wish?' asked the hag.

'I wish to prevent the marriage of King Flan and Princess Emer.'

'Oh!' said the hag, 'come home with me and I shall tell you how that can be done.'

As she said these words she spread out her cloak while still holding the lantern in her right hand. The cloak took the form of two great black wings and the hag flew down to where Maeve stood. Together they went through the wood till they came out at the farther end. There Maeve saw an enormous flat stone lying on the ground. By the far side of the stone a river came hurrying down over some rocks and formed a waterfall. On the side near the wood there was a kind of trapdoor. The hag knocked at this door with a rod of birch which she had taken from a tree as she passed through the wood. Immediately the door flew open and there before them was an ugly old man. He stood at the top of a flight of stone steps which led to a large room beneath. This room was lighted by lanterns hanging on the walls.

'Well, Wife, who is this stranger?' asked the old man.

'Wait till we go down to the room,' said the hag, 'and I will tell you all about her.'

The three descended into the stone chamber. It was cold and bare and the noise of the river at the far end was so great that Maeve feared the water would burst through and drown them all.

When the hag had told her husband what Maeve wished, he said to his wife, 'And what reward will you expect from this woman, if you are able to grant her desire to prevent the marriage?'

'She must get for me the queen's golden mirror and the silver comb of the princess. Then I can comb my hair and keep it from falling into my eyes.'

'And what am I to get?' asked the man.

'I would like the king's slippers because my feet are sore from running up and down the stone steps.'

'Very well,' said the hag. Then she turned to Maeve and said, 'If you promise to get these three things for us, I shall tell you how you can prevent the marriage.'

'But how can I get these things?'

'That you must find out for yourself, but I shall lend you my cloak which will enable you to escape capture if you are pursued. When you have secured the slippers, mirror and comb, hide them safely in your hut. Now listen to my plan for bringing about the death of the princess. Take this pear. It seems to be delicious but inside is a worm which will cause the death of anyone who eats the fruit. If you can manage to get the Princess Emer to eat it, she will trouble you no longer.'

'I will at least do my best to make her eat it,' said Maeve.

'If you fail, there is another way to bring about her death. I know she often sits under a large beech tree in the garden. Take this little axe. It is small but it has wonderful power. Watch till you see the princess coming to sit under the tree. Then strike the trunk near the roots. The tree will fall a short time after you have struck it. You can fly away to safety. The axe can be used only once. It will turn to powder in your hand after you have cut the tree. Now listen to me attentively.'

'I am listening,' said Maeve, 'and I am very thankful for your help.'

'Fearing by some chance,' continued the hag, 'this second plan should fail, I shall tell you of another one. Emer sometimes walks alone by the lake side. Wait in hiding near the deepest part of the water.

Spring out suddenly and push her into the lake. She will be drowned before help can come and your wings will carry you safely away. Now go and return here with the slippers, mirror and comb, after you have succeeded in killing the princess. Take this birch rod. Knock on the trapdoor when you return and it will spring open.'

The old man led Maeve up the steps and the hag brought her through the wood.

All this time the wedding preparations were going on.

Maeve returned to the hut and remained there a couple of days. She stayed inside till the second nightfall and then she went towards the castle to see if she could find some way of getting inside the gates. She noticed that the king and queen with their daughter came out at night to walk in the moonlight.

On the third night after her return, Maeve disguised herself as a beggar woman and went to the castle gates. She waited there for the king and his wife and daughter to come out. She had put on the hag's cloak and under it she carried a bag.

When she saw King Mahon approaching with the queen and princess she crouched down by the castle gates and began to moan and cry.

'Oh! Look at that poor creature,' said the princess.

The king and queen drew near Maeve and asked her what was the matter.

'Oh! Your Majesties,' she exclaimed, 'I am homeless, hungry and desolate.'

'Poor creature,' said the queen, 'we must help her.'

'Here, Fergal,' said the king to one of his attendants, 'take this woman to the kitchen and see that she gets a good meal and give orders to have a bed prepared for her.'

Maeve was loud in her thanks as she followed the attendant. After a while, when all the servants were at supper, she stole quietly to the king's bedroom. There she found the slippers. She put them in the bag. Next she took the golden mirror from the queen's table and then she went to Emer's room and found the silver comb. There was a basket of fruit on the table and in it she placed the pear. She then opened wide the great window and, spreading out the cloak, flew into the night.

When Emer and her father and mother went to their rooms, they were greatly surprised and vexed to find the slippers, mirror and comb were missing.

Emer went to the table to get some fruit and saw the beautiful pear. She was about to eat it when she noticed that the emerald ring had turned black. She opened the pear and saw a horrible worm inside. In fear and disgust she cast the fruit through the open window. When her mother came in to say good night to her, she found her pale and trembling.

'Oh, Mother!' she exclaimed. 'The ring has saved me! I must have an enemy, after all.'

'Who can your enemy be, my child?'

'I believe, Mother, it is that beggar woman. I am sure it was she who left a pear with a horrible worm inside it among the fruit on my table. As I was about to eat it, the emerald turned black and warned me of the danger.'

'Don't be uneasy, Emer; your ring will preserve you from harm.'

Next morning, Maeve kept watch from a hill near the castle to see if Emer would appear. To her rage and disappointment, she saw the princess come out on horseback, accompanied by King Flan.

'She has not eaten the pear,' thought Maeve. She kept a close watch on the castle grounds every day and one morning she saw Emer come out and walk in the direction of the beech tree. She flew at once towards the tree and cut the trunk with the axe. The axe immediately crumbled to dust in her hand. The foliage on the tree was so thick that no one saw her approaching.

Emer came slowly, but when she was a little distance from the tree she saw the emerald turn black. She stood for a moment looking round her, when suddenly she heard a fearful crash and saw the giant tree fall to the earth.

'This again must be the work of my enemy. But for my ring I would have been killed,' she said to her attendant.

Only one chance to kill Emer now remained to the

wicked Maeve. She waited day after day until at last she saw Emer walking alone by the side of the lake. She hid behind some bushes just opposite the deepest part of the water. As Emer came nearer to this point she noticed the emerald becoming darker and darker. She stopped. Maeve sprang from her hiding place, but suddenly she was caught and held fast by a pair of strong arms. Flan had come by a short cut across the fields to join Emer. He saw Maeve crouching down behind the bushes and when she darted out, he followed her and was just in time to save the princess.

The cloak slipped from Maeve's shoulders and to his amazement Flan recognised her.

'At last,' he said to Emer, 'we have discovered who your enemy is.'

'Oh! why have you tried to kill me?' said Emer. 'I have never injured you.'

'We will say no more now,' said Flan, 'but you, Maeve, will come with us to the castle.'

When Maeve was led into the presence of King Mahon and the queen her fear and shame were so great that she confessed all.

'And where now,' asked the king, 'are the things you have stolen?'

'If Your Majesty will have a guard sent with me, I will show you the hut where I have hidden them.'

'That will be done when you have told us where we shall find the hag's dwelling place.'

'It is far from here. First we must pass through a dark wood. The men must take lanterns to light them through the darkest part. At the far end of the wood is the stone dwelling of the hag and her husband.'

That evening Maeve brought the guards to the hut. All the lost articles were recovered. Shortly after the men had returned to the palace a fearful rainstorm came on. In the morning all the streams and rivers were swollen but as the day advanced the weather became fine.

Towards midday King Mahon and King Flan set out for the hag's dwelling, accompanied by a large number of attendants. Flan carried the hag's cloak, for he now knew what magic power it possessed and he feared Maeve would try to fly away.

When they came out of the wood and reached the great stone, the king ordered Maeve to knock on the trapdoor with the birch rod. When she knocked the door opened but inside, instead of the steps and stone chamber, they saw a deep lake.

'Oh, I know what has happened!' Maeve exclaimed. 'The water in the rushing river has broken down the wall at the far end of the chamber.'

'But where are the hag and her husband?' asked the king.

'I am sure, Your Majesty, they have been drowned in the lake and their bodies have been carried away in the rising waters.'

Flan leaned over to look at the lake. The cloak fell from his grasp. Maeve sprang forward to catch it but missed her footing and fell into the depths of the water. She was carried swiftly away by the rushing river. The king and all those with him were shocked to think of her fearful fate. They, like the queen and princess, had forgiven her for all the evil she had done.

In due course, Flan and Emer were married and lived happily ever after.

Emer kept the emerald ring with great care and never parted with it till her daughter Nora was about to be married. Nora in turn gave it to her daughter and in this way it remained in the family as a treasure and a protection against danger.

The Pooka

One lovely summer morning the Princess Eva got up very early and went alone to a large field at some distance from the palace. The dew was still on the grass and the flowers were opening under the rays of the rising sun. Eva sat down on a large stone to enjoy the beauty of the morning. Just opposite where she sat a great number of mushrooms raised their heads among the grass.

All at once she heard singing and then she saw a tiny little boy springing from one mushroom to another. He seemed to be very merry and happy as he danced and sang.

The air of the song was that to which the poet Moore wrote the words 'The Young May Moon', centuries and centuries later.

Eva listened eagerly as the words floated towards her on the morning air:

> 'When sunbeams brighten o'er the sky,
> A merry little fairy, I
> Pass happy hours
> Amid the flowers,
> While weary mortals fret and sigh.'

Just then a field mouse ran out from its nest.

'Good morning,' said the fairy to the mouse. 'Will you try a race with me?'

They started off, but when they had gone a little distance the mouse turned suddenly, ran in front of the fairy and knocked him down, and then scurried back to its nest.

Eva burst out laughing.

When the fairy heard the laughter he ran towards her, turned a somersault and then bowed to the ground.

'It is pleasant to me,' he said, 'to hear a mortal laugh. I am glad you are happy.'

'Who would not be happy at seeing such a bright face as yours?' said Eva. 'Please tell me who you are.'

'Before I tell you who I am, I must ask you a question. Can you keep a secret?'

'Oh, yes indeed.'

'I have heard that no woman can keep a secret.'

'That is not so. I have heard many secrets and I

have never told one of them, though truly, I have heard the same one over and over again from different people who were told it as a secret.'

'But you will tell no one if I tell you who I am?'

'I promise you I will tell no one.'

'Very well. My name is Pooka. Everyone says I am full of mischief but I can be very kind and helpful to those in trouble.'

'Indeed, I am sure you are very good,' said Eva.

'Now,' asked the Pooka, 'have you any secret to tell me?'

'I have a secret. I want to marry a young prince named Niall.'

'And why don't you marry him?'

'My father says he will never consent to my marriage with anyone who is not a crowned king.'

'And won't Niall be a king some day?'

'No, because a wicked, cruel chieftain named Cormac has claimed the kingdom.'

'And Niall is deprived of what really belongs to him.'

'Yes, and he has no one to help him to secure his rights.'

'Perhaps help may come. You see me now as a little boy, but I do not always appear in this form. It will surprise you to hear that I take the shape of a big, black horse at night.'

'Oh, that is very strange,' said Eva.

'Yes, but whether you see me as a boy or a horse, I

can still be your friend. You love the beauty of the morning. So do I. If ever you are in trouble, come here at sunrise and I will help you!'

The Pooka threw his little cap high up into the air, caught it as it fell and then disappeared even more suddenly than he had come.

Eva hurried home.

Now we must hear who she was.

Hundreds of years ago there lived in County Clare a king named Turlough and his Queen Gormley. Eva was their only child. Donough, the king of the neighbouring territory, had just died. Niall, his son, was his rightful heir but Cormac, a powerful chieftain and cousin of Niall's, claimed the throne.

King Turlough, Eva's father, feared Cormac and was anxious to gain his friendship. Queen Gormley thought of a way to bring this about.

'Invite Cormac to the palace,' she said. 'I will have Eva dressed in her most splendid robes and when he sees her in all her beauty he will want her for his wife.'

'That is a great idea,' said Turlough. 'If Cormac and Eva were married, our kingdom would be secure and both kingdoms would be united after my death.'

'I shall go now to Eva,' said the queen, 'and tell her of our plan.'

'You are a wise woman,' said Turlough, 'and a great help to me in all my difficulties.'

The queen went in search of her daughter. She was

told she had gone out alone early in the morning. Now this was the morning Eva had met the Pooka.

'Go,' said the queen to one of her waiting women, 'and bring the princess to me without delay.'

When Eva came into her mother's room, the queen looked on her lovely daughter with joy and pride. Her beautiful, dark hair had been loosened by the morning breeze and her cheeks had the delicate pink of the wild rose.

'You sent for me, Mother,' said she. 'What is your will?'

'I have something of great importance to say to you, my daughter. Sit here by my side. It is time for you to marry and your father and I have chosen a husband for you.'

'Oh, Mother,' said Eva, 'I have myself chosen the man whom I wish to marry.'

The queen looked at her daughter in anger.

'And who is he, I pray?'

'The young prince Niall, who is really the rightful king.'

The king now entered the room.

'This foolish child of ours,' said the queen, 'declares she wishes to marry the young prince, Niall.'

'Nonsense!' exclaimed the king. 'She shall marry Cormac and no other.'

'Listen, Eva,' said the queen. 'We will arrange a great banquet and you will wear your most beautiful clothes and when Cormac sees you he will ask you to be his wife. He is a clever man and will make you a great queen.'

Poor Eva was weeping bitterly.

'I don't want to be a queen,' she said, 'if I cannot be Niall's wife.'

'No more of this,' said Turlough. 'Prepare to meet your future husband, who is Cormac and no other. We will arrange the banquet for tomorrow night. Come,' said he to the queen. 'We will leave this foolish girl to think things over and be ready to do as we wish.'

Poor Eva was very unhappy. She knew her parents would force her to marry Cormac. She had no friend to help her, for she dared not try to see Niall. Then, at last, she remembered the Pooka. Yes, she would steal out before daybreak tomorrow and see him.

The sun was just reddening the sky the next morning when she reached the field. Oh, the joy that came to her heart when she heard the fairy's song!

> 'The bright sun brings another day,
> For me to frisk and dance and play,
> With merry song
> The whole day long
> I while the happy hours away.

'Well,' said the Pooka as he came towards her, 'you are in trouble. I see the sorrow in your face.'

Eva told him all her parents had said.

'And the banquet is arranged for tonight,' said the Pooka.

'Yes,' said Eva. 'Oh, what shall I do?'

The Pooka thought for a while, and then he said: 'Is there anyone in the palace you can trust to give a secret message?'

'Yes,' said Eva. 'My foster mother's son works in the palace. He would do anything for me for his dead mother's sake.'

'Send him to tell Niall to arrive at the palace gates at midnight. Cormac will arrive at the same time and will give something to Niall which Niall is to take from him. Then they are to enter the banquet hall together.'

'But the banquet will begin long before twelve,' said Eva.

'That does not matter. Do as I tell you. I promise you that, with my help and that of my cousin, Will o' the Wisp, all will be well.'

The day was fine but towards evening heavy rain came on and the night was very dark. Cormac, arrayed in all his grandeur, with a splendid crown on his head, set out in his chariot for Turlough's palace. The way lay by the side of a large bog. The night was so dark that the driver feared he would go astray. Suddenly, to his relief, he saw a light shining in the distance.

'That must be King Turlough's palace,' he said as he whipped the horses in the direction of the light. At each step the way became more difficult till at last the horses and chariots stuck in the mud and mire of the wide bog. Will o' the Wisp had lured them out of their path.

Cormac's anger was terrible to behold. He knew he would be late for the banquet. Just then a gentle neighing was heard and the strange light shone on a large black horse standing beside the chariot.

'I am in luck,' said Cormac. 'This horse will take me to the palace.' He sprang from the chariot onto the horse's back and, as he saw neither saddle nor bridle, he caught hold of the long, flowing mane. Cormac tried to turn the horse in the direction of the palace but the animal darted off like lightning through the bog and kept turning and twisting in such a way that the rider could hardly keep his seat. This continued for a long time till they came to a large pool. The horse rose up on his hind legs, threw Cormac off his back and left him sitting in the dirty, black water.

Then, to Cormac's amazement, the horse spoke:

'Unless you promise to do as I tell you,' said he, 'I will bring you to a larger and deeper pool and leave you there to drown.'

Now, Cormac, like all bullies, was a coward.

'Oh,' promised he, 'I will do anything you ask.'

'Very well. You may think it strange that with all the shaking and jumping, the crown has remained on your head. It has done so by my power. I am going to take you to the palace. When you come to the gates, Niall will be there. Take the crown from your head and tell Niall to place it on his. Then walk by his side to the banqueting hall, into the presence of the king and the queen.'

'Oh, but how can I appear before all the nobles with my clothes dirty and dripping?'

'That is part of your punishment for being so covetous and unjust. You must promise before the assembled guests that you give up all claims to the kingdom, which rightly belongs to Niall.'

'I will promise,' said Cormac.

'One thing more,' said the horse. 'If ever in the future you attempt to claim what is not yours by right, I will come for you in the night and bring you here to be drowned in the bog. Now, get on my back and we will go to the palace.... Before we start, I may tell you that the men and horses that were held in the bog are now safely back at your home. The mysterious light which led you astray shone on the chariot and the attendants were able to lift it and the horses out of the mire. The innocent should not suffer with the guilty.'

Off went the horse till it left Cormac at the palace gates when it suddenly disappeared.

Turlough and Gormley, with Eva by their side, welcomed the guests as they came into the banqueting hall. As the night wore on everyone was astonished to find that Cormac had not come. The king and queen were disappointed and angry but Eva felt a great sense of relief.

The feasting and merriment continued until about twelve o'clock when everything stopped short and all eyes were turned towards the entrance door.

Niall and Cormac came in together.

Niall had a crown on his head. He looked very noble and handsome. His cloak was the colour of the purple heather and his tunic as bright and beautiful as the gold of the furze.

Poor Cormac was a sorry sight.

His long, wet hair hung loosely about his mud-covered face, and as he walked up the room the bog water dripped from his torn clothes.

A titter went round amongst the guests.

Turlough rose up in anger and asked why Cormac had dared to appear in such a state before him and his people.

'Oh, King,' said Cormac, 'my present plight is a punishment for the wrongs I have done. I now declare before all the assembly that Niall is the rightful king.'

'What has brought about this wonderful change?' asked Turlough.

'Punishment and shame have taught me how

wrong it was to try to take what did not belong to me,' Cormac replied.

He then turned to Niall and said:

'If you forgive me, I will spend the remainder of my life in helping you in every way I can.'

'I forgive you willingly,' said Niall, 'and in future I shall look on you as my own brother and we shall work together for the good of our kingdom. I assure you I am sorry to see you in this state.'

'I thank you from my heart,' said Cormac, 'and indeed I did not know till tonight that there was so much goodness in the world.'

'Goodness is always to be found if we seek for it properly,' said Eva.

The king now spoke.

'I am rejoiced to find that everything is arranged in such a satisfactory way, and now, to complete the happiness, the queen and I will give our consent and blessing to the marriage of King Niall and our daughter Eva.'

There was great rejoicing at this announcement and the wedding took place soon after.

The morning after the banquet, Eva stole out from the palace and went to the field to thank the Pooka, but he was nowhere to be seen.

Generous fairies, like generous people, demand no thanks for their help or kindness.

Cliona's Wave

A loud noise, as from the surging of a wave, is occasionally heard in the harbour of Glandore, County Cork, both in calm and stormy weather. It is the forerunner of the shifting of the wind to the northeast. It is called the 'Tonn Cliona' or Cliona's wave and was supposed to portend the death of some great personage.

King Turlough and his Queen Sive had their palace near Glandore, in County Cork. They were married many years and had no children. At last a beautiful baby girl was born. She was called Ethna and was the joy and pride of her parents' hearts.

One lovely day the king and queen were seated at a window in the palace, looking at the beautiful scene that lay before them.

'Cloudless sky and sparkling sea,
Cliff and shore and forest tree,
Glen and stream and mountain blue,
Burst at once upon the view.

'Who would not be happy,' said Turlough, 'while looking on such a scene?'

'Well, you and I are certainly very happy,' the queen replied, 'and it is a joy to think that little Ethna is heiress to all this beauty. There she is, sleeping peacefully in her cradle under the hawthorn tree, with her faithful nurse by her side.'

'Sometimes,' said the king, 'I wonder if the nurse is so faithful. It has been whispered to me that she cares more about Fergus, the gardener, than she does about our little Ethna.'

'Oh, don't mind those idle rumours,' the queen said. 'I am sure she is very attentive to the child. Let us walk down to the sea. It is a pity to be indoors on such a day.'

'Look how calm the water is,' said the king. 'It is almost without a ripple, except where the wavelets break on the beach.'

'Yes, but there is a swell on the sea and the wind is turning to the northeast.'

Suddenly, a loud noise was heard, a noise as from the surging of a wave. Both Turlough and Sive trembled and turned pale.

'That is Cliona's wave!' cried the king in great alarm.

'Yes,' said the queen, 'the wave that gives warning that some terrible sorrow is to come to us. Can we do nothing to lessen the fairy's power?'

'Alas, no! No one is strong enough to lessen the power of the fairy, Cliona.'

They returned in haste to the palace. Everything there showed signs of trouble and confusion.

'Oh, what has happened?' cried the queen.

There was silence for a moment and then Turlough and Sive were told that their dear child was lost. The nurse had left the baby sleeping under the hawthorn tree and had gone some distance away to speak to the gardener. When she returned the child was gone. She had been stolen by the fairies.

'I knew,' said Turlough, 'that some great sorrow was coming to us when we heard the sound of Cliona's wave.'

'Oh, why,' asked Sive, turning to the nurse, 'did you leave our child alone?'

'It is just as if she had died,' said the king, 'for we shall never see her again.'

From that time happiness and peace were gone from the palace. Sorrow and gloom reigned in their stead. Years went by without bringing any tidings of Ethna. Turlough and Sive tried to rule wisely and to look after the welfare of their subjects, but they never ceased to pine for the child they had lost.

One day Sive was walking along a road just outside the palace when she saw a woman and a little boy coming toward her. As the woman drew nearer, the queen saw that she looked very tired and ill. In a moment she had fallen to the ground. One of the queen's waiting women hurried into the palace to call for help. When the woman was brought in, it was found that she was dying.

She whispered to the queen: 'My husband, who was a chieftain in a territory some miles east from here, was killed when defending his home from his enemies. I travelled here to ask you to befriend my little Donal when I am gone.'

In a few moments the woman was dead.

The queen felt it was her duty to take care of the little boy. Gradually she came to love him as if he were her own child. She and the king determined to make him their heir. They often spoke to him of Ethna and it became the great wish of his heart to bring her back to her home.

Years passed and Donal grew to be a fine, handsome youth. He was as good as he was handsome. He had a great love of the sea and used to go many miles from land in a boat which the queen had given him. Sometimes he would take provisions with him and would spend hours on the water.

One warm August day when the sea was like a beautiful spreading lake under a blue sky, Donal ventured farther and farther from the shore. As he went southward, he saw in the distance a small island. It seemed to be covered with emeralds and rubies. As he drew nearer, he saw that rows of rowan trees grew round the coast. Their foliage and berries were what he had thought were gems glistening in the sunshine.

A little cove faced him as he approached the land. He made fast his boat and went in on the island. From the trees came the sound of human voices and, to his amazement, he found that these voices belonged to birds perched on the trees. Numbers of birds were there, brown, black, green and other colours, all chattering away in human speech.

While Donal was wondering at what he saw and heard, he noticed a strange-looking house in the centre of the island. It was built of stone and had a long, sloping roof.

The birds continued to talk. Donal lay down on the sward near the house and listened to them.

'Yesterday,' said the pigeon, 'I flew to Glandore Castle and rested in the hawthorn tree in the garden. The king and queen were sitting under the tree. They were speaking sadly of the Princess Ethna who was carried away to fairyland many years ago.'

'They will never see the same Ethna again,' said the raven in a harsh, croaking voice. 'The fairy Cliona holds her a captive in her court.'

'Oh, you always have the worst news!' exclaimed the thrush.

'Well, I know what I am talking about,' retorted the raven.

'Peace, peace,' said the gentle voice of the dove.

'Yes,' said the little wren, 'let us be bright and cheerful.'

'Was Ethna the name of the princess?' asked the swallow from her nest under the roof of the house.

'Yes,' replied the pigeon, 'Ethna was her name.'

'Well, then I know where she is. In the spring, when we swallows were coming back to Ireland, we flew over a fairy fort some miles north of Glandore. I stopped to take a sip of water from a river nearby. I saw a mortal maiden in the fort and heard the fairies call her Ethna.'

Just then Donal saw a boat approaching the island. An old, bent man came on shore.

'You are the first visitor that has come to my island home,' he said to Donal, 'and I bid you welcome.'

Donal thanked him and told him he had been much interested in listening to the conversation of the birds.

'Yes,' said the old man, 'these birds see and hear a great deal in their flights from the island and, as they have the gift of speech, they tell me everything that happens.'

'I have heard very important news from them,' said Donal.

'What is that news?'

'It is about the Princess Ethna, who was years ago taken from her father's home by the fairies. The birds say she is in Cliona's fort.'

The old man shook his head.

'Cliona has wonderful magic powers and, even if you could reach the fort, it would be difficult to rescue the princess. I can help you, however, if you are brave enough to attempt to bring Ethna back.'

'I would do anything to restore her to her parents.'

'Well, then I will give you all the help I can but there will be difficulties and hardships in your way. Cliona's fort is several miles north from Glandore. I will send the pigeon to be your guide by day and the owl to lead you at night.'

'But how will I know the place?' asked Donal.

'You will come to a great rock in the middle of a circular space. Round this rock is a row of smaller stones. This place is *Carraig Cliona*, that is Cliona's rock. It is useless to approach the fort by day. Wait for a moonlight night.'

'The moon is full at present and I should like to reach the fort tomorrow night.'

'You can do that if you return home now and set out in the morning.'

'I will take the fastest horse in the stable,' said Donal.

'No,' said the man, 'you must go on foot. When

you have travelled about twenty miles, you will come
to a little house half-hidden by trees. I will send one of
my birds to tell the woman of the house to expect you.'

'But how shall I succeed in freeing Ethna from the
fairy's spell?'

'That will not be easy. Cliona is very clever. She
can take the form of different animals. She can
become a deer, a hound or a rabbit but whatever
shape she assumes, her green eyes remain the same.
Before you set out on your journey tomorrow, cut a
branch of the hawthorn tree in the palace garden, a
branch with berries on it. If you can manage to strike
Cliona with the branch, you will have her in your
power and she must do as you wish.'

'And how shall I find Ethna?'

'Command Cliona to call her forth and the
princess will gladly come. Do not on any account
enter the fort yourself. You must not eat, drink nor
speak from the time you leave the island till you reach
the house among the trees. Now take my blessing and
hasten away.'

As Donal sailed from the shore, the birds sang in a
chorus:

> 'Happy will the princess be,
> When young Donal sets her free,
> He will break the cruel spell,
> And the fairy's power will quell.

May kind fortune on him smile,
As he leaves our wooded isle.'

Everyone in the palace had retired to rest before
Donal returned. The night was warm and he slept in
a summer-house in the garden. Early in the morning
he went to the hawthorn tree to cut the berried
branch. There, sitting on the top of the tree, was the
pigeon which was to be his guide.

As Donal travelled on, the day became very hot
and he felt tired, hungry and thirsty. He saw a woman
coming toward him. She had a basket full of delicious
fruit in one hand and a glass of mead in the other.
She offered him the fruit and mead. Donal longed to
take them but he remembered he must not speak, eat
nor drink. He gave one longing look at the good
things, shook his head and passed on.

When he had gone a little distance he looked back
to the place where he had met the woman but she
was nowhere to be seen, though that part of the road
was quite straight, without bend or turning. The
pigeon acted as his guide till he reached the house
among the trees. Then the bird turned and flew
southward. To his great surprise, he saw, standing at
the door of the house, the woman who had offered
him the food and drink.

'You are heartily welcome,' she said.

Donal thanked her and followed her into the house.

'You have bravely borne hunger, thirst and weariness,' said the woman, 'and now you will have your reward.'

She led Donal into the room where a delicious meal was prepared for him. When he had finished his meal she told him to go into the inner room.

'There is a bed,' she said, 'where you can rest till you hear the owl's cry.'

Donal was glad to rest and soon he fell into a deep sleep. He was awakened by the hooting of the owl. He went to the window and by the light of the moon saw the bird on the branch of a tree. As he was leaving the house, the woman said to him:

'If you succeed in your effort to free the princess, there will be food and rest for both of you here on your return journey. Take this horn,' she said, 'and blow it three times when you reach the fairy fort. Cliona will then appear before you.'

Donal again thanked the woman and followed in the direction in which the owl flitted from tree to tree. He came in sight of Cliona's rock. He blew the horn once, twice, three times. Out from the fort walked Cliona. She was very beautiful but there was a cruel gleam in her green eyes.

As she came near to where Donal stood, he attempted to strike her with the hawthorn branch. Immediately, she changed into a white rabbit and ran round and round the court. Then darkness fell. Donal felt something descend on his shoulder. It was the owl whose voice whispered in his ear:

'I will tell you when the rabbit is coming close to where you stand and will warn you when to strike....'

'Now,' said the owl, after a few seconds.

A piercing shriek was heard. The darkness cleared away and Cliona stood there, weeping and wringing her hands.

'Command the Princess Ethna to come forth,' said Donal.

'Come, Ethna, come,' called Cliona, as she herself disappeared into the fort.

From the centre of the court Ethna approached the surrounding rocks. She stepped outside and looked around her in wonder and joy.

'Oh,' she exclaimed, 'what a beautiful world! But where shall I find the loving friends I have so often seen in my dreams?'

'Come with me,' said Donal, 'and their joy will be greater even than yours when you are all reunited.'

The owl led them back to the little house where the woman gave them a warm welcome. When they were departing on their homeward journey she said to them:

'There will be great rejoicing in the palace when you return and soon there will be a happy wedding there.'

The king and queen wept for joy when they saw

their loved child again. Everyone in the palace shared in their delight.

The woman's words came true, for Donal and Ethna were married almost immediately after their return and lived happily ever after.

The Wishing Chair
(A Story of the Olden Time)

'We are a happy family,' said Shane MacFadden, as he and his wife and daughter Róisín were having their supper one fine summer evening.

'Yes, indeed, Shane,' said his wife, 'but you have to work hard to keep us in such comfort.'

'You know, Nora, I am well helped by you and Róisín.'

'And, Father,' said Róisín, 'you also have managed to give me a good education and the opportunity to learn to play the harp.'

Róisín gave much pleasure to her parents by playing for them in the long winter evenings.

They were indeed a happy family with no thought

of the trouble that was to come to them.

Sickness broke out in the neighbourhood. The inmates of the little house did not escape. Both father and mother died.

Róisín recovered. A sad and lonely girl she was.

Her aunt, who lived some distance away, said she would leave her own house and come with her two daughters to live with her.

'I will be a mother to you, Róisín,' she said, 'and Mella and Gobnait will be just the same as sisters.'

It was a sad day for Róisín that the three women came to the house. All three were lazy and idle. They left all the work to Róisín.

The two girls were always arguing and quarrelling.

'I am tired of this life,' Mella said one day. 'I wish some handsome, rich man would come and marry me.'

'You with your yellow face and long, lanky figure the wife of a rich, handsome man!' said Gobnait.

'Well, Gobnait, I would rather have my nice, slight figure than be a fat, heavy creature like you. It is well you have such huge feet for if they were small they would never support your big, bulky body. If you did not eat so much you might have a nice, slight figure like mine.'

Róisín tried to make peace between them.

'You would both be much happier if you did not quarrel so much,' she said.

'Oh, you need not talk, Róisín,' said Mella. 'Everyone loves you.'

'Yes,' added Gobnait, 'and with your beauty you prevent anyone from looking at either of us. You were lucky, too, in having had such devoted parents and in getting a good education.'

'Our parents took very little care with our upbringing,' said Mella. 'Even now my mother does not bother about us. She is either dozing at the fire or talking to the neighbours.'

There was neither peace nor comfort in the house and Róisín was very unhappy.

One night the sisters were looking out the window while their mother was sitting at the fire. Róisín was trying to tidy the kitchen.

'There is the new moon,' said Gobnait. 'I see it clear in the sky and not through a tree. Perhaps it will bring me good luck.'

'I don't care about the moon,' was Mella's remark. 'It never brought good luck to me.'

'Oh, look!' exclaimed Gobnait as a woman passed by the window, 'there is Ana Críonna [wise Ana]. I will call her in. She has always plenty of news.'

The woman, as her name implied, was believed to be very wise. She had wonderful stories of the olden time. For miles round she was welcomed in the different houses, but she never stayed longer than a couple of days in each.

'*Céad míle fáilte* [a hundred thousand welcomes], Ana,' said Róisín as she placed a chair near the fire.

'Though the day was warm the evening is chilly,' said Ana, 'and for an old woman like me the heat is pleasant.'

'Well, Ana, what news have you tonight?' asked Gobnait.

'Good news,' Ana replied, 'there is a new owner in Dunbawn Castle.'

'That is the castle,' said the mother, 'where the rich widow lived. She pined away after the death of her beautiful daughter Maeve.'

'Yes,' said Ana. 'The new owner is the widow's nephew. He is the last of the family and will inherit all the wealth.'

'What is his name?' asked Gobnait.

'Brian is his name. He is a fine, handsome young man.'

'And who will live with him in the Castle?' asked Mella.

'Oh! there are many attendants, but the principal one is Nuala, his old nurse. She has been with him since he was born. Both his parents have been dead for some years. I must be going now, for I have some distance to walk to the next house.'

'Oh, Ana, don't go till you tell me my fortune,' said Mella.

'And mine,' said Gobnait and Róisín, speaking together.

'Now, girls, I cannot tell you your fortune, but I can tell you how to get good luck for yourselves. I am doing this for your sake, Róisín.'

The three girls gathered round her, anxiously waiting to hear what she would say.

'Your face is your fortune, asthore,' she said to Róisín, 'but it is your kind heart that will bring you the good luck.'

Ana smiled as she said:

'Now listen, girls. You all know the high bank at the back of the strand near the Black Rock.'

'Yes,' came in a chorus.

'If you climb the bank you will come to a field. Walk through the field to the stone fence at the end.'

'Is it a long field?' asked lazy Gobnait.

'Yes, and when you have crossed the fence you will come to another field, a larger one.'

'Must we walk through that too?' asked Mella.

'Yes. And when you have crossed the fence at the far end you must walk through another field, much larger than either of the others.'

'Oh! I could never do that,' said Gobnait.

'Well, if you could not, it is useless for me to tell you any more.'

'Oh, go on, Ana,' said Mella. 'Don't mind lazy Gobnait.'

'Yes, go on,' said Gobnait, 'perhaps I could try the long walk.'

Ana continued:

'At the end of the third field there is a little wood. The trees form a kind of circle. In the centre of the circle there is a stone chair. This is the Wishing Chair. Anyone who sits in it can wish three times. In this way they can get three things which they desire.'

'I'll start off in the morning,' said Gobnait.

'No,' said Ana. 'You must go in the order of age. Mella first, then Gobnait and then Róisín. I must leave you now. I wish you all good luck. Good night.'

'I'll get up at cock-crow in the morning,' said Mella.

'You will,' laughed Gobnait, 'if the cock begins to crow at midday. That is your usual time for rising.'

'You are not such an early riser yourself,' was the angry retort from Mella. Turning to Róisín, she said: 'You call me when you yourself are getting up.'

Next morning Mella left the house at an early hour. She walked briskly to the sea shore. When she reached the high banks she thought she would hardly be able to climb to the top of them. She made a great effort but by the time she had crossed the third field she was exhausted and parched with thirst.

With lagging steps, she came to the little wood. As she sat down in the chair she forgot everything but her desire for a drink. She cried aloud, 'Oh, how I wish I had a drink of clear, cold water.' Immediately the leaves on the trees overhead seemed to sing the words, 'Your wish will be granted.'

There at her feet she saw a well of sparkling water and a vessel at the brink.

She took a long drink and then remembered that one of her wishes was gone.

'My second wish is that I will have roses in my cheeks like the lovely colour that Róisín has in hers.'

Again the leaves seemed to sing —

'Your wish will be granted.'

All at once nice pink roses appeared in her cheeks, but there were thorns in each which pricked her.

'Oh!' she cried, 'my third wish is that these thorny roses will go away. Bad as my yellow face was it did not hurt like this.'

The voices in the leaves answered —

'Your wish will be granted.'

The water in the well turned yellow and in it she saw her face reflected.

'You don't look very happy,' said Gobnait as her sister reached home, weary and footsore.

'Never mind how I look,' snapped Mella.

'Well,' said Gobnait, 'I will try my luck tomorrow and I hope I will come home happier than you are after your adventure.'

Next morning, Gobnait rose early. She ate a good substantial breakfast, for she had always a great appetite.

Her experience was much the same as her sister's till she reached the wishing chair.

The fresh air made her very hungry.

'I'm starving,' she cried out. 'I wish I had a good dinner.'

The voices in the leaves called out —

'Your wish will be granted.'

There beside her, on a crystal tray, she saw a delicious meal. She ate heartily. Then she remembered that one of her wishes was gone.

'My second wish is that I will have a nice slight figure instead of being so fat and bulky.'

The voices in the leaves said —

'Your wish will be granted.'

Thereupon she felt her body shrinking and shrinking till her clothes hung so loosely round her that she looked like a long pole. Her feet seemed now to be enormous under her thin, lean body.

'Oh,' she said, 'I wish I had my own figure back again.'

Again came the song in the leaves —

'Your wish will be granted.'

All at once her own appearance returned.

She went home and ate a fine supper. Then she went to bed and tried to sleep off her disappointment.

On the third morning, Róisín got up very early. She left everything in order for the three lazy women who were still sleeping.

After a hasty meal she set out for the Wishing Chair.

The beauty of the morning made her glad. The sea was calm and sparkling under the golden rays of the sun. As she went through the fields she stopped for a moment to gather some of the wild scabious that grew on the borders of the fields. All was calm and peaceful in the brightness of the lovely summer day.

Still it was a weary girl that reached the Wishing Chair. She sank down on the chair, worn out for want of food and rest.

Unconsciously she called out —

'I wish I could rest and slumber a while.'

The voices in the leaves sang —

'Your wish will be granted.'

Suddenly she was asleep and dreaming. In her dream she saw a tall, handsome man. He smiled at her and seemed about to speak. While still half-dreaming, she exclaimed —

'Oh! how I wish that such a man as that would be my husband.'

The voices in the leaves sang —

'Your wish will be granted.'

'My third wish is that I will soon have a home far away from my aunt and cousins.'

The voices in the leaves answered —

'Your wish will be granted.'

She began her return journey. After having walked about a mile she heard a cry from a small tree by the wayside. As she stopped she saw a bird hanging from one of the branches. A thread or hair had evidently got entangled in its foot. She climbed up the bank where the tree grew and set the captive free.

The bird flew to a neighbouring tree. It chirruped gaily, as if to thank the friend who had given it its liberty.

As Róisín was descending from the bank she came upon a large stone and hurt her foot badly. When she tried to walk she found she could not move without severe pain.

Her home was far distant and very few people came along the way. To add to her troubles her dress had got badly torn.

Poor Róisín was in despair. She sat down by the wayside and cried. After a while she heard the sound of approaching footsteps. Round a bend in the road a woman came into sight. To her relief and delight she saw her friend Ana Críonna coming towards her.

'What is the matter with my *cailín dílis* [my dear girl]?' were Ana's first words.

While Róisín was telling her friend all that had happened, a sound of wheels was heard. Round the curve came a splendid carriage drawn by two fine horses.

Ana rushed forward and stood in front of the carriage. It stopped. The door was opened by the footman. A young man alighted. Róisín looked at his face and uttered a cry. She would have fallen if Ana had not caught her as she became unconscious.

The stranger was the man she had seen in her dream.

Ana recognised him as Brian, the new owner of Dunbawn Castle.

'Oh! Sir,' said Ana, 'have pity on this poor girl. She has hurt her foot and is not able to walk.'

'Where is her home?' Brian asked.

'A good distance from here, if indeed it can be called a home for there will be small comfort when she goes there.'

Róisín had now partly recovered consciousness.

'Will you come with her if I take her to my home?' asked Brian.

'Gladly will I go. I would do anything for the girl I love so well.'

Turning to Róisín she said —

'Come now, my girl, good fortune has sent a carriage to bring you to a nicer place than the home you have left.'

Still in a half-swoon, Róisín was helped into the carriage. Ana sat beside her and talked cheerfully, telling her all would be well.

The carriage stopped outside a splendid castle. When the door was opened an elderly woman with a kindly face came forward to meet Brian.

'I have brought visitors, Nuala,' he said.

Róisín, half dazed with wondering, was led to the door.

'Well, my son,' said Nuala, 'if kindness and beauty are recommendations, the visitors have certainly a big share of both.'

She led them to a fine room and placed Róisín on a comfortable couch.

Brian came into the room and soon Nuala had heard the whole history of the meeting.

'I must go to some friends I promised to see this evening,' said Brian. 'I will not be back for some days. Will you, Nuala, take care of our guests till I return?'

'That I will do and welcome,' said Nuala. 'Indeed it will be nice to have someone young in the house.'

Soon Róisín was in a comfortable room with a dainty meal placed before her. Ana shared the meal and cheered the patient with the interesting things she had to tell her.

'Now, Róisín,' said Nuala, 'rest for a while. Ana and I will have a little chat.'

When the two women were talking together, Nuala said —

'I have taken Róisín to my heart. Her beautiful fair hair and blue eyes remind me of my dear boy's cousin Maeve. I will be lonely when she leaves.'

A far-away look came into Ana's eyes as she said, 'Yes, when she leaves.'

Gradually the sprained foot improved until Róisín was able to walk without trouble.

'Now, Ana,' she said, 'since I am able to walk

again I should return home. I fear I have outstayed my welcome by remaining so long.'

'Oh, alanna,' said Nuala, 'don't think of going until my dear boy comes back. He would never forgive me if I let you go without seeing him again. What do you say, Ana?'

Ana paused and looked very wise. Then she said, 'My advice is that Róisín stays.'

There was now the question of dress to be considered as Róisín's own had been so badly torn.

'Will the pair of you come with me to Maeve's room?' asked Nuala. 'There are many dresses there which the poor girl never wore.'

Ana was lost in admiration of Róisín when she saw her arrayed in a magnificent dress.

'I always knew you were beautiful,' she said, 'but you now look like some wonderful creature from fairyland.'

'Perhaps,' said Nuala, 'you would like to see the different rooms in the house.'

'Oh, yes,' was the answer from both.

'Here,' said Nuala, 'is the room where poor Maeve used to play the harp.'

'Oh, may I play, please?' asked Róisín.

'Of course, asthore, and welcome. Come, Ana, and I will show you the other rooms.'

Róisín forgot everything in her delight in the music. She played on and on and did not notice that the door of the room had been opened until she heard a voice say, 'Maeve.' She turned round and saw Brian standing in the room.

'I fear I have startled you,' he said. 'For a moment I thought my cousin Maeve was back again. Please continue to play.'

Róisín was unable to play. She felt as if she were again in the Wishing Chair dreaming of the handsome young man who now stood by her side.

Ana and Nuala came into the room. 'Now,' said Ana, 'I can start on my travels again. The roving life suits me best.'

'I wish you would stay, Ana,' said Brian, 'but I understand your longing to return to your old way of life, but I want to ask you to leave Róisín with us.'

'Oh, yes, Ana,' said Nuala, 'please leave Róisín with us.'

'Won't you stay, Róisín?' asked Brian, 'and stay always, for from the moment I first saw you I knew you were the girl I would like to make my wife.'

'And perhaps later on,' said Ana, with a knowing smile, 'she will tell you of the first moment she saw you.'

Nuala took Róisín in her arms, saying — 'Oh, we will now have a happy home. My dear boy won't be lonely any more.'

'But my aunt and cousins!' said Róisín.

'Your aunt and cousins!' exclaimed Ana. 'If ever they attempt to come near you I'll get all the bad fairies in the country to plague them day and night. *Slán agaibh* [good-bye] now. My next visit will be for the happy wedding.' With these words she hurried off.

The wedding was one of the grandest ever seen in the countryside and Brian and Róisín lived happy ever after.

Asailín

One cold winter's night, Jack Kenny, his wife and family were gathered round a blazing fire in their comfortable kitchen. Jack was glad to rest after a hard day's work on the farm. His wife was sewing while her foot rocked the cradle where Billy, the youngest child, lay.

Peter was learning his lessons for the next day while Katie tried to teach the alphabet to Annie and Nora. Suddenly a sound was heard from outside the door. A sort of cry or snort followed the sound. The father opened the door. 'Oh! What strange thing is this?' he exclaimed. 'Peter, get the lantern.' The light of the lantern showed a thin, miserable ass lying on the ground.

'Oh!' said Peter, 'that is poor old Mickey Rourke's

ass. I know it by the bald spot on its head. Mickey used to say the ass got a cut on his head and the hair never grew on it again.'

'I suppose,' said the mother, 'the poor animal got nothing to eat since Mickey died more than a week ago. Indeed sometimes it was little the old man himself had to eat.'

'Father,' said Katie, 'what will we do with the ass?'

'I think, Katie, we can't do much for it. I would say it will hardly live till morning.'

'Couldn't we lift it off the cold clay and put it in the shed?' asked Peter.

'Yes,' said Katie, 'and leave a bit of hay and some clean water near it.'

'Have your way, children,' said the father, 'but I don't think the poor beast will last through the night.'

Just then, a neighbour, big Jim Horan, happened to be passing by. With his help, the ass was brought into the shed. Peter ran for a vessel of water and Katie got some nice clean hay.

'Well,' said the mother, 'that is all we can do for poor Mickey's ass.'

Next morning Peter was in a nice, sound sleep when he was awakened by these words — 'Get up, Peter, and come with me to see if the ass is still alive.'

'It is hard to get out of my comfortable bed, Katie, but if you go and open the door of the shed, I'll follow you.'

'All right, I have the lantern, for it is still dark, and there is no one awake in the house but ourselves.'

When the children went into the shed they found to their delight that the ass was still alive.

'Look,' said Peter, 'I think he has eaten a bit of the hay. Maybe he will get strong and we can have him for our own.'

The father and mother were surprised when the children told them of their experience in the morning. Later on, the mother herself went to the shed with some oats. This the animal ate with some relish. After a few days he was able to walk about. The fact that the children had cared for him so well made them wish to keep him.

In a short time he was a fine sturdy animal. His intelligence was quickened and strengthened by the love the children had for him.

'We must give him a name,' said Katie, 'and let it be an Irish one.'

'I remember,' said Peter, 'poor Mickey when driving the ass used to say, "Now, Asailín, off we go." Let us call him Asailín.'

Asailín was now a big, handsome donkey.

'He is a fine sturdy brute,' said the father, 'but we don't really want him. He is of no use on the farm.'

'Oh, Jack,' said the mother, 'he may not be much use but the children love him and he loves them. We can't judge things for their use only. If we did what would we think of the primroses and cowslips?'

'You are right, Mary; the fact that he adds to the children's happiness is service in itself.'

Some of the neighbours' children used to enjoy rides on Asailín. There was a boy called Bobby Martin among the group. He was not as kind as the others. He liked to tease Asailín. One day he brought him a bucket full of dirty, bad-smelling water. Of course, Asailín refused to drink. Worse than this, another day he tied an old tin can to his tail. This last act caused so much anger among his companions that he was not allowed to join in the play any more.

The children arranged to have a sports day with Asailín. Each child was to ride on him round the field without bridle or saddle. The one who did the round in the shortest time was to get the prize. Bobby asked to be allowed to join in the game.

'No,' came in a chorus, 'he will not be allowed.'

'He was cruel to Asailín,' said Peter, 'and should not be let take part in the game.' Bobby began to cry. Kind-hearted Katie was sorry for him.

'Let us give him a chance,' she said. 'I am sure he will be kind to Asailín from now on. Won't you, Bobby?'

'Yes,' said Bobby in the midst of his sobs.

The children, one by one, mounted the ass. He ran round the field with each and seemed to enjoy the sport. Bobby was the last to mount. Asailín started off but quickly went off the track to a corner of the field where there was a large stagnant pool. When he reached the pool he raised up his hind feet, and poor Bobby found himself sitting in the dirty water.

On Christmas morning the father asked the children would they like to go to the stable to wish Asailín a happy Christmas.

'Oh, yes, yes,' came the answer from all. When they reached the stable, their delight was unbounded. There was Asailín yoked to a lovely little car.

'Oh, Mother,' said Peter, 'I can now drive you into the village to get the provisions and all you want from the shops.'

Time went on and the ploughing season arrived. The father took the two horses and went some miles away to a friend's house to help in the work.

'I will be back the day after tomorrow,' he said as he was going off.

Night came on and all the children were in bed. The mother had many little jobs to do. She was just finishing up her work when she heard a scream from the cradle. She lifted the baby. He seemed to stiffen in her arms. His cry wakened Katie and Peter.

'Oh, Mother,' said Katie, 'I think poor Billy has convulsions. He looks like Julia Dolan's child that died last year. I was in the house when the doctor came. He said he could have saved the child if he had been called in time.'

'Oh, what will we do?' said the mother. 'Your father has the horses and no one will be able to get the doctor in time.'

'Mother,' said Peter, 'I'll yoke Asailín and we will reach the doctor's house in no time.'

When Peter reached Dr O'Toole's house he, by good luck, found the doctor getting out of his car.

'Oh, Doctor,' Peter said, 'will you come quickly? Our baby will die if you do not come at once.' The good man did not hesitate. He jumped into his own car and was soon in the house where he was to bring such relief.

'Mrs Kenny,' he said, 'I am only just in time, but don't be uneasy, we will save the little fellow.' Billy was his bright little self after a few days. When the father reached home he heard all that had happened. 'Now, Jack,' said his wife, 'you see how useful Asailín has been. He was the means of saving Billy's life.' Asailín lived to a ripe old age and remained to the last the friend and loved companion of all the family.

The Magic Mist

Time: Long, long ago.
Place: A fine mansion near the coast of Donegal.

One lovely summer morning, Fergus, the owner of the mansion, was seated at breakfast with Una, his wife, and their daughter Aideen. There was a beautiful view to be seen from the castle. The gardens, trees with the deep blue sea in the distance formed a lovely picture.

'I believe,' said Aideen, 'that Ireland is the most beautiful country in the world.'

'I agree with you,' said her mother. 'I am sure my dear old friend, Nessa, will be pleased to return to it. She and Ronan, her son, will arrive here today.'

'Has she been long abroad?' asked Fergus.

'Yes, she went away shortly after her marriage but since her husband's death she has been longing to return home.'

'How old is her son?' asked Fergus.

'He is in his early twenties.'

'Then he is some years older than Aideen.'

'Yes, I am sure both mother and son will be happy with us here in Ireland.'

After a short time the guests arrived. Una and Nessa were delighted to meet again. Fergus and Aideen listened with interest to Ronan's accounts of his travels.

'You have been in many countries,' said Fergus.

'Yes, and from what I have seen of Ireland I think it is very beautiful.'

The day passed pleasantly. Towards evening, all five went out to sit in the lovely garden. The visitors were entranced with the beauty of the evening as the golden sun sank over the sea.

Suddenly, a strange figure appeared. It was that of a tiny woman. She had small eyes like black beads and a strange expression in her rather wrinkled face.

'Will you give me one of your beautiful golden locks?' she asked as she looked at Aideen's lovely hair.

'How dare you intrude on us and make such a request,' said the father angrily.

'Hush, my dear,' whispered the mother as she turned pale. 'It is a fairy that has spoken.'

The little woman disappeared as quickly as she had come. Una was trembling as she said to her husband — 'Oh! why did you speak so harshly to that woman? She has it in her power to do us great harm.'

'Nonsense! What harm could a miserable little creature like that bring to us?'

'Father,' said Aideen, 'I have heard that the fairies have great power, and that they take bitter revenge on anyone that angers them.'

'Yes, my dear,' said the mother, 'they can reward or punish according to the treatment they receive from us mortals.'

'Again I say nonsense. You both are too ready to believe in the power of "the good people" as they are called. Certainly, if that woman is a sample of their goodness I would not like to meet many of them.'

All at once a heavy fog spread over the castle and the surrounding grounds.

'This is not an ordinary mist,' said Una. 'I fear some wicked fairy power has brought it on. We had better go into the house at once. Will you, Fergus, take care of Nessa? Ronan can come with me. I know Aideen will find her way alone.'

The fog became more dense. They groped their way along till they reached the house. Then to their surprise and alarm they discovered that Aideen was not with them. The fog cleared almost as quickly as it had come but though a thorough search was made through house and grounds Aideen was not to be found.

'The fairies have had their revenge,' said Una.

Macha, Aideen's old nurse, was as much grieved as were the parents.

'Oh! Macha,' said the distracted mother, 'can you think of any way in which we can find our loved child?'

Macha thought for a moment. 'Here is my advice,' she said. 'Consult Eagna, the wise druid who lives in the house by the side of the Silver Stream.'

'How clever you are, Macha,' cried Fergus, 'I am sure Eagna will come to our aid.'

The druid arrived. He was a tall man. His appearance and bearing were such as to inspire trust and confidence. He listened attentively to all the details concerning Aideen's disappearance. 'The fairies can be bitter enemies,' he said. 'The magic mist is one of their most powerful weapons and one which is hard to combat.'

'Is there any hope that we will recover our lost child?' asked the father.

'Yes, if one very important factor can be procured.'

'Oh! what is that?' asked Fergus. 'I will give all I possess to find Aideen.'

'Wealth will be of no avail,' said the druid. 'What is needed is a valiant champion who will face all harm and danger for her sake.'

'But where will such a champion be found?' asked Una.

'If,' said Ronan, 'my efforts would avail I will do anything in my power to find the missing girl.'

'Well spoken, my dear son,' said his mother.

'Remember,' said the druid, 'that if you undertake the work of bringing the girl safely home you must act with speed, cleverness and bravery.'

'Well, I shall do my best to restore Aideen to her parents. Please give me instructions as to how I should proceed.'

'Here are my directions,' said Eagna. 'At the place where the Silver Stream enters the sea there are huge rocks. High up among them is a strange cave-like dwelling. The inmate of this place is as strange as the dwelling itself.'

'I have heard of her,' said Fergus. 'She is called "the Hag of the Rocks".'

'Yes, but be careful never to speak of her by that name. She calls herself the "Beauty of the Rocks" and if anyone wishes to please her or to seek her help the best way to succeed is to address her by that name.'

'From all I have heard of her,' said Fergus, 'she is anything but a beauty.'

'Well, what you have heard is true but it is also true that she will not help anyone unless her beauty is praised.'

'Will that praise be enough to secure her help?' asked Una.

'Oh! no, she will set three tasks to be done before she will give any help.'

'What are the tasks?' asked Fergus.

'Three things — Anyone seeking her aid must first play some musical instrument, second, sing a song in her praise, third, tell a story.'

'You, Ronan,' said his mother, 'can certainly supply the music.'

'Mother, I could not take my harp with me.'

'No, but you can take your silver flute.'

'Good,' said Eagna. 'Now what about the song?'

'Oh!' said Ronan, with a laugh, 'it will be easy to compose a verse or two about her beauty.'

'Now the story,' said Eagna.

'Surely, Ronan,' Nessa said, 'you remember some of the stories I told you when you were a child.'

'Never mind, Mother dear, I will tell a story which will please the witch.'

'Now,' said the druid, 'a few more words of advice and warning. It will be difficult to climb up the rocks that lead to the witch's home. Rub your hands on the grass that grows on the side of the Silver Stream. You will gain strength from this and will be able to hold on to projecting stones. Have a boat moored at the mouth of the Silver Stream so as to be able to take Aideen safely home.'

'I, myself,' said Fergus, 'will give orders to have the boat moored in time.'

'I shall now depart,' said the druid. 'May good fortune attend you all.'

'Please wait till I order the carriage,' said Fergus.

'Thank you,' was the druid's reply, 'but I prefer to walk by my beloved stream and enjoy the beauty of the night.'

Thanks and blessings were accorded Eagna as he left the castle. 'Be sure to bring your flute, Ronan,' said Nessa.

'You need not fear, dear Mother, that I will forget any of the directions which the kind druid has given me.'

The moon was shining brightly when Ronan reached the place described by the druid. From the directions given him he was able to ascend to the witch's home. The house looked like a sort of beehive with a small door in the centre. The witch heard him approaching and was standing at the open door.

'She is certainly no beauty,' Ronan thought, as he looked at her little wizened face and scraggy hair.

She spoke — 'What brings you to my rock-built home?'

Ronan answered in rhyme. 'To seek your help, fair one, I've come.'

The witch seemed pleased with this answer.

'Now tell me what you wish me to do for you,' she said.

Ronan gave a full account of the disappearance of Aideen. The witch thought for a while. 'I can help you to find the girl,' she said, 'but before I render any assistance you must please me by performing three tasks.'

'I will gladly do as you command,' was Ronan's answer.

'The first task is that you play a sweet tune.'

Ronan took out his flute.

'If the tune is as fine as the instrument I will indeed be pleased,' said the witch.

Ronan played a lovely, sweet sad air. Tears came into the old creature's eyes as she listened.

'Good, good,' she said. 'If your performance of the other two tasks is as good as that of the first, I will surely grant your request with pleasure. Now for your song.'

Ronan had a lovely voice. Gazing at the witch he sang these lines:

> 'To worth and beauty
> It is my duty
> With homage due to bend the knee
> Be not afraid
> To lend your aid
> And I shall ever thankful be.'

The witch was even more pleased with the song than with the music.

'Now,' she said, 'I will ask you to tell me a story. It must be short and have an element of fun in it as I like to be amused.'

Ronan cleared his throat and swelled out his chest. 'My story,' he said, 'has no beginning and, therefore, can have no end.' The hag laughed heartily. 'You have earned your reward,' she said. 'I will now tell you how you can rescue the stolen girl. First of all you must have a boat moored at the mouth of the Silver Stream.'

Ronan knew that the boat would be ready but he did not mention the druid's name.

'Now listen carefully,' said the witch. 'Some distance from here there are two islands, one larger than the other. On the larger one the fairies have their home. On the other Aideen is in captivity. Row quickly to the smaller island. Take the girl into the boat. The fairies will hasten to take to their boats and follow you.'

'Are they not sure to overtake us?' asked Ronan.

'Not if you follow my instructions. Wait a moment and you will understand.'

The hag mounted on a piece of rock and took from a small opening in the wall a thick roll of what looked like strong cord.

'Now,' she said, 'when you are getting into the boat take hold of the end of this cord. Keep pulling it along and keep a firm grasp on it even after you have reached the island and have Aideen in the boat. I will be here on the shore waiting for a signal from you. When you are ready to start on your homeward way give a chuck to the cord. I shall then know when to pull the end of the cord which I have kept and which will be a line of communication between you and me.'

Ronan followed the hag's instructions. The boat sped swiftly over the sea. All was quiet on the islands. Poor Aideen was standing near the edge of the water looking wistfully towards her home. Soon she was in the boat and sailing homewards, but the fairies had seen her depart and had followed the fugitives.

'Oh! they will capture us and sink the boat,' cried Aideen.

'Have no fear,' was Ronan's reply as he pulled the cord and gave the signal to the hag who was waiting on the shore.

Like lightning the boat sped over the water and left the fairies far behind. The hag was on the shore waiting to welcome them.

'Now give me back my magic cord,' she said.

'With my heartfelt thanks,' said Ronan.

'And mine,' added Aideen.

'We meet now,' said the hag, 'only to part for ever. My power can be used once only for each friend.'

Ronan, to please and thank her for the service she had rendered, sang for her a little song.

'Oh! lovely creature
In form and feature
With grateful hearts we offer thanks
To one so clever
Whose brave endeavour
O'ercame the fairies' wiles and pranks.'

The poor old hag almost cried with joy as she disappeared.

It would be hard to describe the delight of all who welcomed home the happy pair. Their joy was complete when some time after there was a splendid wedding. Ronan and Aideen married amid great rejoicing and lived happy ever after.

Airne
(The Sloe Fairy)

The Fairies

All the graceful spirit people,
children of the earth and sea
Whom in days now dim and olden
when the world was fresh and golden
Every mortal could behold in
haunted rath and tower and tree.

Denis Florence MacCarthy

Long, long ago there lived in the North of Ireland a poor widow named Sorcha. Her house was in a lonely glen which was surrounded by mountains. She had one child, a boy four years old. Diarmuid was his name. He was not strong and his poor mother was unable to procure the nourishment he required.

There was a small patch of land round the house. A blackthorn tree grew in the centre of it. The tree was surrounded by what was believed to be a fairy ring.

Sorcha would never allow the sloes to be gathered nor the daisies in the ring to be pulled. She believed they belonged to the fairies.

Her entire means consisted of the patch of land, a goat and some fowl. The only playmate Diarmuid had was a dog named Madra. There was great love between the animal and the child.

Sorcha's house was very small. It contained but one apartment. Diarmuid slept in a corner near the fire. Madra slept on the floor beside him. The mother's bed was in the other corner. The fowl and the goat were both taken in at night.

Sorcha had a friend named Bríd who lived at some distance from her. A kind, generous friend she was.

'Indeed, Sorcha,' she would say, 'I wish I could give you more meal but it is hard to get enough for my big family and their father.'

'You are very kind and good, Bríd, to give me all you do. I could manage better only for the fierce giant who lives at the other side of the mountain. He comes now and again and takes every bit of food that is in the house. If I refuse to give him the food he threatens to take Diarmuid away.'

The women spoke in low tones so as not to waken Diarmuid who was asleep in his little bed.

'Poor Sorcha!' said Bríd. 'I wish I could help you. You are alone in this valley with no one near you except your delicate child.'

'Even if there were other people near me who of them all would be strong enough to fight the fierce giant? He has a big bag of stones fastened at his belt and he throws them at anyone that comes near him.'

'Yes,' said Bríd, 'and if he caught anyone, one blow of his huge club would mean death.

'Well, Sorcha, I must go now, but I will come again as soon as I can. *Slán leat.*'

After a little while Diarmuid wakened.

'I am hungry, Mother,' he said.

'Well now, *a mhic*, here is a nice bit of porridge for you.'

'Was Bríd here?' asked Diarmuid.

'Yes, and she brought some meal.'

When Diarmuid had finished his frugal supper his mother took him on her lap and began to tell him a story.

Suddenly Madra uttered a growl.

Heavy footsteps were heard outside and then the giant's terrible voice saying, 'Fee, Faw, Fum. Open the door or I will break it in with my club.'

Poor Sorcha knew she would have to open the door. The giant entered. He was awful to behold. His red beard reached to his waist. His eyes were like burning coals. His ears hung down on his shoulders.

'Now,' said he, 'give me all the food you have in the house.'

Sorcha handed him what was left of the meal that Bríd had brought her.

'This is a very small amount,' said the giant. 'I will come again tomorrow night and if you have not more for me I will take your child. He is thin and small but he will make a meal.'

Scowling at mother and son he departed.

Sorcha tried to soothe and comfort the frightened child but she herself could not keep back the tears.

When Diarmuid was asleep Sorcha went out to get water from a well which was near the house.

Just as she had filled her pitcher she heard at a short distance the sound of a sweet voice.

She stood still and listened.

These are the words that were sung:

> 'Free from sorrow, free from fear
> All your woe will disappear
> If you let this stranger here
>   Come into your home.
> The giant you will fear no more
> Safe will be your house and store
> Listen, open wide your door
>   And let the stranger come.'

Sorcha remained standing as if in a dream. Then she walked on.

There beside the blackthorn tree stood a tiny woman. She was dressed in white. A large jewel on her breast shone so brightly that Sorcha could clearly see her beautiful black hair and sparkling eyes. Round her neck was a necklace made of daisies.

Sorcha looked at her in wonder.

Then the woman spoke.

'My name is Airne [Irish for sloe].

'I am the sloe fairy. Bring me to your home. I will save your child from the cruel giant.

'I will do this because you have always respected the blackthorn tree and its fruit as well as the daisies that grow round it.'

Sorcha led the way to the house.

'The giant will come tomorrow night,' said the fairy.

'Yes, and he said he would take away my child if I had no food to give him.'

'Don't fear. I will befriend you.'

The fairy took a slender rod from out the folds of her dress.

'This wand,' she said, 'is from the fairy sloe tree. It has magic power. Now, when you hear the giant approaching strike the three animals with it. The goat will become a bellowing bull, the dog a fierce wolf and the cock a screaming eagle. They will all three approach the giant. He will run in terror from the house.

'When he is safely out of the way touch the animals again with the wand. They will resume their natural shape.

'When this is done the wand will turn into smoke and pass up the chimney.

'Now I charge you not to tell anyone I have been here. Farewell.'

Like a flash the fairy reached the door and disappeared.

Sorcha found the next day very long and dreary. There was no food in the house, other than a few eggs.

Night came on. Diarmuid went asleep. Sorcha waited in fear, fear mingled with hope.

At last the awful voice was heard. 'Fee, Faw, Fum. I want my supper. I hope the boy is ready.'

Diarmuid wakened and lay trembling in the bed.

Sorcha, though shaking in every limb, prepared for the attack. She struck the goat, dog and cock with the wand.

Then she opened the door.

The giant rushed in. He stood still, stupefied.

The bull, bellowing loudly, bent down and knocked the club from his hand.

The wolf uttered a fearful growl and showed his teeth.

The eagle flew up above his head and flapped his wings over his eyes.

Terrified and almost blinded, the giant rushed from the house.

Sorcha struck the three creatures with the wand. They immediately resumed their own forms.

The wand turned into smoke and disappeared up the chimney.

The giant climbed the mountain in great haste. When he was descending on the other side he missed his footing. He was unable to halt. He fell down, down until he plunged into the lake at the foot of the mountain.

Down he sank into the depth of the water till his body was buried in the mud at the bottom.

Now who should be passing near the lake but Sorcha's friend Bríd. By the light of the moon she saw the giant falling into the lake.

She uttered a loud scream that was heard by the inmates of a carriage which was approaching.

A man and woman alighted from the carriage. They were Fionn and Fidelma, who lived in a great castle some distance away.

'What is the cause of your alarm?' Fionn asked.

'Oh! I saw the giant of the mountain falling into the lake,' Bríd answered.

'It would be useless to attempt to rescue anyone from that lake. The giant's life is over,' said Fionn.

'Can nothing be done?' asked Fidelma.

'Nothing, there is no such thing as anyone returning from the Lake of Doom, as that water is called.'

'It was a terrible death,' said Fidelma.

'Yes, my dear, but the giant himself was a terror to the neighbourhood. You yourself have lost some of your most precious possessions by his fierce and constant robberies.'

Turning to Bríd, Fidelma asked:

'Did you ever hear of the giant?'

'Indeed I did and there is a friend of mine who was much troubled by him.'

'Where does your friend live?'

'In a little house in the glen. She is very poor and has a delicate child.'

'What is her name?'

'Sorcha is her name. She lived in constant fear of the giant. He threatened too to take the child if she did not get him more food.'

'I wonder could we help this poor woman and her sick child,' Fidelma said to her husband.

'We will talk about these things later on,' he replied, 'we had better return home now.'

'I will go to Sorcha's house later on,' said Fidelma to Bríd as the carriage moved away.

Bríd stood for a moment looking after it. 'I am sure poor Sorcha has found a friend,' she thought.

Then she hurried off to the little house in the glen.

'I have news for you, Sorcha,' she said. 'The giant will trouble you no more. He has been drowned in the Lake of Doom. Here is a little bread for your supper.'

'Will the giant never come again?' said a small voice from the bed.

'No, Diarmuid, alanna,' answered Bríd, 'so go to sleep now. Your mother and you are quite safe. Good night, Sorcha, and happy dreams.'

When Fionn and his wife returned home they sent out word to their friends that the giant was dead.

He had been a terror to all in the neighbourhood.

There were few houses from which he had not stolen some precious and valuable things.

Fionn and some others who had been robbed by the giant set out to find his home.

After a search they discovered a sort of cave at the foot of the mountain. In it were all the treasures he had stolen.

The owners took each one his own share.

When all the stolen goods had been distributed Fidelma said to her husband:

'You remember the woman we met the night the giant was drowned.'

'Yes,' replied Fionn, 'Bríd was her name.'

'She told us about a poor woman who lives in the glen. The woman that was persecuted by the giant.'

'Yes, I remember.'

'Well, tomorrow morning I will go to the glen and see that woman and her sick child.'

'Yes, that is the right thing to do. You may be able to help her.'

Next morning Fidelma went to Sorcha's house.

The door was open. She stood still for a moment outside.

Sorcha was sitting with her child on her lap. Her friend Bríd stood beside her.

'Oh! Bríd,' said the poor mother as the tears fell down her cheeks, 'I am afraid he is going from me. The poor child did not get the food that would keep him well and strong.'

Bríd could not answer. She, too, was crying.

Fidelma went into the house.

For a moment all three were silent.

Then Fidelma spoke.

'This is the house you spoke of the night we met you at the mountain,' she said to Bríd.

'Yes,' said Bríd, 'and this is my friend, Sorcha.'

Fidelma looked with pity on the weeping mother and her child.

'Don't fret,' she said. 'Your child will get all the nourishment he requires. He will be soon well and strong. Will you, Bríd, remain here till I return? I will not be long away.'

She hurried out to her carriage and after a time returned with an abundance of food.

'You must not remain in this little house,' said Fidelma. 'There is a nice home near the castle. We will bring you there. Your neighbour, too, must be rewarded for her kind help.'

'Oh!' said Sorcha, 'I would not like to leave this house. I came to it with my poor husband and we spent many happy days here.'

'But for your child's sake will you not come?'

'There is another reason why I want to stay here. I would not like to leave the blackthorn tree and the daisy ring.'

'Then,' said Fidelma, 'if you are determined to remain here we must erect shelters outside for your goat and the fowl.

'You, Bríd, can continue to help Sorcha for I will get some extra land for you and put cows there.'

'Oh!' said Bríd, 'then I will be able to give milk to Sorcha and Diarmuid.'

'For the future,' said Fidelma, 'I shall see that neither of you will want for anything.'

Fidelma kept her word.

Both women were made comfortable and happy in their homes.

Diarmuid grew strong. As the years went by he was able to work hard and was the joy of his mother's heart. The house was enlarged and mother and son enjoyed peace and comfort.

The fairy never appeared again but the blackthorn tree and the fairy ring were still regarded as the most precious possessions of mother and son.

The Three Fires

Long, long ago in what is now County Cavan there lived a king called Fergus.

In his youth he had been handsome, clever and wealthy but indolence and extravagance had robbed him of his power and possessions.

'I have but a short time to live,' he said to his three grown sons who stood by his bedside. 'I am now glad that your poor mother died so many years ago. Though she knew ruin was coming she did not see the worst.'

'Indeed,' whispered Niall, the eldest son, to his brother Art, 'she would have lived longer if care and anxiety had not caused her early death.'

'True,' replied Art, 'but you and I are also to blame. We followed closely in our father's footsteps.'

'Hush,' said Brian, the youngest son, 'perhaps Father will hear you. Don't make things harder for him.'

The father spoke again.

'My sons,' he said, 'you know I cannot leave you wealth or means. I don't know how you will live.'

'Don't fret about us, Father,' said Brian, 'as long as the wealth lasted we had a good time. We must now face the future with hope and courage.'

'Call Lughai, my faithful old druid,' said the King, 'perhaps he will be able to give you some help. Indeed he himself is not far from death but I know he will do all in his power to save you from complete misfortune.'

Brian hurried from the room.

After a short time he returned leading in a feeble, old man.

'I have sent for you, Lughai,' said the King, 'to ask you can you do anything to help the poor sons whom I have brought to ruin.'

'I will, my beloved King, use the last of my druidical powers on their behalf, but they must follow exactly the directions which I shall give them.'

Turning to the sons he said:

'Say good-bye to your father and come with me.'

As the brothers led Lughai from the room he turned to the father and said:

'Farewell my King. Both you and I will pass away with the setting sun.'

With difficulty the sons led the druid to the top of a little hill which was near the castle.

Everything was bright and peaceful in the calm of the evening.

'It is hard to leave such beauty,' sighed the druid.

He took from his belt a branch of yew and pronounced some incantations on it.

'I will send each one of you on a journey,' he said.

Then turning towards the north he struck the side of the hill with the branch of yew.

Immediately a stream of fire came forth and passed very slowly down the slope.

Turning towards the south he repeated the action.

Again a stream of fire trickled down.

He performed a similar rite on the eastern side with the same result.

'You see, my friends,' he said, 'I have left the west untouched for I myself shall travel down that track and pass away with the sunset.

'Now listen carefully to what I have to say.

'Follow these streams until the fire ceases to burn. You must not stop nor rest until it disappears. On no account turn to look behind you. If you do you will be drawn back here. No matter what sounds you may hear keep looking on before you. Now, Niall, you are the eldest. I will give you your choice as to in which direction you will go.'

'My answer is this,' said Niall.

'I'll choose the north and may it be
A good and lucky choice for me.'

'You, Art,' said Lughai, 'in what direction will you go?'
Art answered at once,

'Towards the south with hope and speed
I'll travel where the fire will lead.'

'You are the last, Brian,' said the druid, 'but perhaps
your good fortune will be none the less for that.'
Brian with a good-humoured smile replied,

'No choice is left me but to go
Straight towards the east for weal or woe.'

'Now, my friends,' said Lughai, 'I will remain here till
I see you depart. Listen and heed my warning:

Hasten now, make no delay
Nor once look backwards on the way.'

As the three brothers turned in different directions the
druid went slowly down the hill under the rays of the
setting sun.

When he reached the foot he lay down and fell
into a deep sleep. He never wakened. Just at the same
time the King died. No one was at his bedside but
Síle, the faithful attendant who had loved the poor,
suffering Queen.

The brothers travelled on but gradually they
became tired and longed for rest.

As Niall was plodding onwards he heard the sound of trampling feet behind him.

In alarm he forgot the druid's warning. Looking round he saw a huge figure with its hand raised as if to strike him. The figure disappeared as quickly as it had come but the stream of fire turned and Niall found himself dragged back to his own home.

Art, like his brother, travelled on till he heard the trampling feet behind him. Nearer and nearer came the sound. In terror he looked round. He saw the same figure as his brother had seen. As it disappeared the stream of fire turned and by some unseen power he was forced to follow it towards his own home.

Brian was the bravest and the strongest of the three but even he was becoming weak and exhausted.

He heard the trampling feet. Closer and closer came the sound. Weary as he was he began to run. The footsteps hurried too. In the midst of his haste and fear he still remembered the druid's warning, 'Don't look back.'

Just as his strength was failing the fire went out.

He sank down almost unconscious on the green sward opposite a great castle. All was still and silent under the bright light of the moon. Suddenly he heard a voice saying, 'You have acted well and bravely. You will get a great reward.'

He looked around but even in the bright moonlight there was no one to be seen.

He heard the voice again.

'If you continue to be brave and faithful good fortune will be yours.'

Then he heard a slight noise close beside him. As he looked he saw a dark cloak lying on the ground. Standing beside it was the shadowy form of a fairy.

She spoke. 'I am from the fairy host. My cloak makes me invisible. My special charge is to care for the inmates of the castle. From the fairy fort I saw the druid's fire and watched it disappear. Then I knew someone had followed it.'

'I followed it from my father's castle,' said Brian.

'Yes, and you have been wise and brave for I know the wicked wizard tried to lead you astray.

'You see that great castle yonder?'

'Yes,' said Brian, 'who lives there?'

'A chieftain named Cormac with Ina his wife and Cliona, his daughter. They do not know what danger is threatening them.'

'Can they not be warned of the danger?'

'Warning would be useless. A huge, fierce giant will be coming to the castle tonight to steal away the princess.'

'Can nothing be done to prevent him from carrying her off?'

'Yes, something can be done and you are the one to do it.'

'But I have no weapon.'

'We will talk of that later on. First you must eat and drink for you have had a hard and trying time.'

The fairy led Brian to a field where an apple tree grew beside a pond.

'The fruit of this tree,' she said, 'and the water of the pond have special qualities for satisfying even great hunger and thirst.'

After having eaten and drunk Brian felt quite strong and refreshed.

'Now for your task,' said the fairy. 'There is only one way to successfully fight the giant.'

'What way is that?' asked Brian.

'If he is wounded in the right eye he will die immediately.

'Now, pluck that one apple which is on the lowest branch of the tree.'

'It is very hard,' said Brian, 'and it is as small as a hazel nut.'

'Yes, but it is the only weapon that can overcome the giant. Tell me, have you a steady aim?'

'Oh! yes, I can hit any target. Long practice in playing with my brothers has made me perfect, but how can I aim properly with no light but the light of the moon?'

'There will be light from the castle because the screams of the princess will waken all the household. Sit on that large stone yonder and rest till midnight. The giant will then appear.'

The fairy then put on the cloak of darkness and vanished.

Brian was weary and though he tried to keep awake he fell into a deep sleep.

At twelve o'clock the giant reached the castle. He went in by the back entrance. One blow from his huge club burst open one of the doors. All in the castle were asleep. The giant went straight to the room of the princess. Her scream awakened everyone in the castle, but before help could reach her the giant had carried her outside the front entrance.

Brian had fallen into a heavy sleep but the noise from the castle wakened him.

He was just in time to see the giant outside the door with the princess in his arms.

'Stop,' he called as he made ready to hurl the apple.

The giant burst into a fit of laughter.

He laid the princess on the ground and turned towards Brian brandishing his club.

Quick as a flash Brian hurled the apple. His aim was perfect. The giant fell lifeless to the ground.

Cliona remained unconscious for some time after she had been brought back into the castle.

Her father and mother watched by the couch where she lay. Brian stood beside them.

After some time she revived.

'Oh! where is the giant?' she asked.

'The giant will never trouble you again, asthore,' said the mother.

'This brave man,' said the father as he looked at Brian, 'has slain him. We owe our safety and peace to him.'

Brain declared the happiness was all his that he had been able to be of some service and help.

'Won't you be our guest for some time at least?' asked the mother.

'Oh! Yes,' said Cormac, 'stay with us and prolong the friendship so strangely begun.'

Brian hesitated.

'Do please, stay,' Cliona said.

This remark removed all doubt from Brian's mind. Indeed he was very glad to remain in the castle.

After breakfast next morning Cormac asked Brian to go out with him to see the place round the castle.

When the two men had left the room Cliona said:

'I wonder, Mother, who the stranger is.'

'Whoever he is, Cliona dear, he is a brave and good man.'

'And Mother, don't you think he is very handsome?'

'Indeed I do. He looks to me like the son of a king.'

Brian felt he should not trespass on the hospitality of his new friends, yet he hated to depart.

When night came and all was quiet he stole out into the calm, still air.

Just near the apple tree he heard the voice of the fairy.

'You followed my directions before with success. Now listen to further ones. Tell the story of your life to Cormac. All will then come right. Farewell, we shall meet no more.'

Brian recognised the voice but the fairy had remained invisible.

Next morning he told Cormac who he was and how he had come to the palace.

'Yours was a hard fate,' said Cormac. 'You deserve better than that which seems to be in store for you. My advice to you is that you stay with us for some time.'

'Thank you for all your kindness but I think it is better for me to depart at once.'

'Why must you hurry so?'

'I will tell you the truth,' said Brian, 'the longer I stay the harder will it be for me to part with your beautiful daughter.'

'To part with my daughter! Please remain here at least till I return.'

While this conversation was going on Cliona and her mother were walking together in the flower garden.

'Won't the house be very lonely, Mother,' said Cliona, 'when Brian leaves?'

'Yes,' said the mother, 'and we do not know where he is going. We may never see him again.'

Tears came into Cliona's eyes.

Just then her father came into the garden.

'Why such a sad face, Cliona?' he said.

The mother answered the question.

'She is sad because she fears that when Brian leaves she may never see him again.'

Cormac smiled.

'After all the suitors she has rejected she has now given her heart to a stranger.'

'Father, he saved my life.'

'Well, come Ina, come Cliona with me.'

He led them to the room where Brian awaited him.

'You have told me, Brian,' he said, 'that the saddest thing in your parting with us here is that you must leave Cliona.'

'Oh! I have not said those words,' said Brian.

'No, not exactly those words, but I understand you will be sorry to part with her.'

'But,' began Brian —

'Wait a moment, please,' said Cormac.

'Cliona has had many suitors. Not one of them would she accept. Now she is very sad at the thought of parting with you. Why not the pair of you marry and be happy?'

'But,' said Brian, 'I am poor and in no way worthy of such a wife.'

Here the mother spoke.

'Brian,' she said, 'Cormac and I are most anxious

that Cliona will marry. There will be no one to care for her when we are gone.'

'As well as that,' said Cormac, 'we want our great possessions to be in hands such as yours.'

There was a lot more talk but the end of all was that a marriage was arranged between the young pair.

There was a splendid wedding.

The handsome pair were radiantly happy.

After some time Brian told Cliona and her parents that he would like to get some tidings of his brothers.

'I would like to know what has been their fate.'

'I can well understand that,' said Cormac. 'Let you and Cliona travel westwards and seek them.'

'But,' said Ina, 'do not remain too long away. We shall be anxious if you are not back in a short time.'

With some attendants the pair set off in carriages drawn by their best horses.

'We must rest on the way,' said Brian, 'for the journey is long.'

It was night when they reached the castle. It was dark and deserted.

'There is a light in that house opposite the palace,' said Cliona.

'Please, let me go alone to the house and make enquiries,' said Brian.

He uttered an exclamation of surprise when the door was opened by Síle, the loved and faithful attendant of the whole family.

In her delight she threw her arms round Brian as she called out, 'Oh! come and see who is here.'

In answer to this call Niall and Art appeared.

'Oh! Brian,' said Niall, 'we thought you were dead.'

'He is far from being dead,' said Art. 'Look how well and grand he is.'

'Where have you been?' asked Niall.

'Wait till I call my wife and then we can hear and tell everything.'

The brothers and Síle were surprised and delighted to see the beautiful young wife.

Niall and Art were silent for a moment but Síle said —

'Oh! tell us where you found so lovely a girl.'

Brian told them of his adventures and of all that had happened.

'And now,' said he, 'tell me why the castle is deserted and you are all living in this house.'

'It is a very nice house,' said Cliona.

'Yes, alanna,' Síle replied, 'but a poor one for my boys.'

'Don't say that, Síle,' said Niall. 'We are happy and content here. Now, listen to what had happened. When the fire drew us back we knew we could not again live in the castle. There was no one there but dear, faithful Síle.

'We had no means and no friends.'

'Oh!' said Cliona. 'Were you very sad and lonely?'

'Yes, for a time, but this house was empty and we determined to work out a living for ourselves.'

'Yes,' said Art, 'and make atonement for the useless and extravagant lives we had led.'

'But how do you work out a living?' said Brian.

'The land round the house is rich. We produce our own food. Síle looks after us with the greatest care and we feel we are living useful lives at last.'

'We are well fed,' said Niall, 'well housed and have peace and plenty.'

Síle gazed lovingly at Brian.

'Oh, *a mhic mo chroí*, when I look at you I think I see your mother's bright, blue eyes.'

'Brian has lovely eyes,' said Cliona.

'Yes, a cushla, but not lovelier than your own.'

'We must leave you now,' said Brian.

'Oh, why so soon?' asked Art.

'We have a long journey before us and we promised Cliona's parents that we would not be long away. However, I go with a light, happy heart now that you are well and contented.'

'I would not change my life to become a king,' said Art.

'Nor I,' echoed Niall.

Síle left the company for a moment. She returned carrying some vessels.

'You must not go till you take a *deoch an dorais*.'

'Yes,' said Niall, 'will you please us by taking a

drink of mead? Among other activities we keep hives of bees.'

'May we come to see you often?' asked Cliona.

'Oh! Yes. There will always be *céad míle fáilte* for you here,' came as answer from the brothers.

'And,' said Brian, 'we will come soon and take you all three for a visit to our happy home.'

Jack and his Animals

Years and years ago there lived in that part of Ireland which is now County Tyrone a man named Lorcan with Bríd his wife and Jack their only child, a boy in his teens.

They had been happy and fairly comfortable till the father lost his health. He had worked very hard to provide a good home for his wife and child but his health broke down under the strain of the hard labour.

Jack was a kind, loving boy. As he grew older he felt he should find some means of helping to make life easier and happier for his parents.

He was very fond of animals and had wonderful power in training them and winning their affection.

'Mother,' he said one day, 'I have thought of a plan to make life easier and more comfortable for you and my father. We have four animals here, the ass, the dog, the cat and the goat.'

'Well, Jack alanna, what do you mean to do?'

'You know, Mother, I have trained the animals to play tricks and I have thought that perhaps I could earn money by amusing the people who would see them performing.'

'Certainly, Jack, you have done extraordinary work in teaching the beasts. Not only do they perform wonderfully but they also enjoy the play.'

'Well, Mother, I will start on my travels at once and I promise you I will return home as soon as possible.'

Jack made all things ready and set off. He took his fife with him.

The parents stood side by side at the window of the room where the poor invalid passed his days. They waved a loving farewell to their good son.

He, with the four animals, travelled on till they reached a field near a small town.

Jack placed the animals in a row, took out his fife and began to play. Immediately the four responded to the music. The ass began to bray, the dog to bark, the cat to mew and the goat to bleat.

In a little while most of the people in the neighbourhood assembled in the field to listen to the 'band'.

After a short time Jack stopped playing. Immediately the animals followed his example.

One old lady, a lover of animals who had been brought out to witness the performance, gave orders to have a good meal prepared at her house for Jack and his animals. Both man and beasts thoroughly enjoyed the food. She also gave Jack a good sum of money.

Jack wished to derive as much profit as possible from the long day.

He gathered his band together and started off to go to another town. When they reached it he arranged the animals in order on a patch of waste ground.

The music started. In a short time it seemed as if all the people of the town were gathered together to hear and see the strange band. The animals themselves seemed to enjoy the game.

Among the crowd was a rich man named Feilim, with Finola his wife and Maeve their seven-year-old daughter.

'Father, where are the man and the animals going now?' Maeve asked.

Jack himself answered the question. 'We will travel a bit farther and reach a wood. We can sleep under the trees.'

'Oh!' said Feilim, 'rain might come on and you would have no shelter.'

'There is a big empty shed near the back of our house,' said Finola. 'The animals could sleep there. You yourself can find a bed in the house.'

Both Jack and his animals slept comfortably that night. They started off early next morning after having a good breakfast.

Feilim with his wife and daughter stood at the gate of the house to say goodbye. Maeve had been given a purse of money to put into Jack's hand. He was delighted to think of the joy the money would bring to his parents.

He travelled on till he came to a splendid mansion surrounded by trees. It was the home of a wealthy chieftain named Angus, Anna, his wife, and their daughter, Eva.

They had been for years a very happy family but were now a sad one.

Eva was a beautiful girl and was as good as she was beautiful.

A marriage had been arranged between her and a fine young chieftain named Oscar.

All preparations had been made when a sad occurrence put an end to the joyful anticipation.

One lovely spring day Eva and two of her companions, Bríd and Siobhán, went for a walk along a winding road known as the Witch's Lane.

It was so called because a wicked witch had her home there among the bushes and brambles.

The witch was feared by the people of the neighbourhood. It was said she put cruel spells on anyone who dared to go near her dwelling place.

When the three girls came towards it Siobhán and Bríd turned back but Eva went on.

'I am not afraid of the ugly old creature,' she said.

She had gone only a very short distance when the hideous old hag rushed out from among the bushes.

She had a crooked stick in her hand.

With it she struck Eva on the mouth as she said:

> 'Power of speech you'll ne'er regain
> All help and cures will be in vain
> Till strange, quaint music greets your ear
> And drives away all doubt and fear.'

Laughing and cackling the witch rushed back towards her den.

In her savage delight she forgot the deep lake near her home. She stumbled over a large stone. In vain she tried to reach the brambles. The water seemed to drag her down, down. She was never heard of more.

Her wicked power had put poor Eva under a cruel spell. She was deprived of the power of speech.

Oscar wished the marriage to take place as arranged but Eva herself would not consent to such an arrangement.

Jack happened to select for his next performance a field near Eva's house.

The day was bright and sunny. The birds were singing and the blossoms were sprouting on the trees. Scenes of beauty and renewed life appeared on all sides.

Angus, his wife, daughter and Oscar were seated at the midday meal when they heard the sound of extraordinary music.

Eva loved music. She rushed without ceremony from the table and hurried to the place from whence the sound had come.

The parents and Oscar followed her. All four were amazed to see Jack and his band. The sight was a fantastic and funny one.

The poor donkey was getting tired but he kept on bravely with his part so as to hold his place in the orchestra.

The dog kept on changing the key from threatening growls to barks of joy and welcome.

The cat mewed loudly but now and again softened the tone to a gentle purr.

The *meg-geg-geg* of the goat was somewhat nasal but was constant and well sustained.

The parents and Oscar listened for a moment to the 'choir' but what was their joy when they turned towards Eva and saw that she was laughing heartily.

'Oh! Father, Mother, Oscar,' she cried, 'the cruel spell is broken. The witch's prophecy has come true. Strange, quaint music has been my cure.'

All the listeners came forward with generous money gifts.

Angus asked Jack what were his plans for the future.

'I will go home now to my parents,' was his reply.

'Is your home far from here?'

'Well, it is a good distance.'

'Oh! then we must find some means of sending you back.'

'Do you remember, Father,' said Eva, 'there are wagons in the stables that would take more than twice the number of animals? And Jack himself could be sent home on one of the side-cars.'

The triumphant march home began. Jack received a tumultuous welcome from all his neighbours and friends.

With great care and good food the father regained his health and both people and animals lived happy ever after.

The Well at the World's End

King Conor and Queen Eithne had one daughter named Noneen, who was beautiful and good. Noneen's nurse, Aoife, lived at the palace, also, and her daughter Maeve and the little princess often played together.

One day Queen Eithne became ill and after a few days she died. Before she died, she called the nurse, Aoife, to her and begged her to take care of Princess Noneen and King Conor always. Aoife promised that she would, but she never meant to keep that promise, because she was a wicked woman.

One day Aoife went to the old witch who lived on Grass Mountain and asked her what would be the best way to get rid of Princess Noneen.

'I will tell you what to do,' said the witch. 'Send

Noneen up here to my cave tomorrow. Give her a basket and tell her to bring you back a dozen eggs. I promise you, she will not go back to the palace alive.' And the old witch laughed shrilly. 'No,' she continued, 'she won't go back alive; but don't let her take any kind of food with her, for if she does, the spell will be broken.'

Aoife thanked the witch and went down the mountain to the palace. Next morning Aoife called Princess Noneen to the kitchen.

'Will you take this basket and go up to the witch of Grass Mountain for some eggs?' she said. 'I haven't even one and you know how your father likes an egg for his breakfast.'

So Noneen took the basket and set out for the Grass Mountain. On her way she felt hungry, because she had had no breakfast. She searched her pockets to see if she could find anything she could eat. All she found were some cake crumbs and she ate these.

She came to the witch's cave and asked for the eggs. The witch gave them to her and as Noneen was walking away, the old woman tried to cast a spell on her. The spell did not work and so the witch knew that Noneen must have eaten something.

Aoife was very surprised and very angry when she saw Noneen back safe and sound, but she pretended to be glad and said, 'Good girl, Noneen; I hope you didn't break any of the eggs. You can have one for your breakfast. Did you eat anything at all yet?'

'Only a few crumbs I found in my pocket,' she said.

A few days later Aoife again asked Princess Noneen to go up to Grass Mountain for eggs and this time she turned out Noneen's pockets before she left the palace.

Noneen felt hungry on the way because she hadn't yet had breakfast and when she saw some juicy blackberries on a bush she picked some and ate them.

When she reached the cave on Grass Mountain, the witch again tried to cast a spell over her, but as Noneen had eaten the blackberries, the spell didn't work. She got the basketful of eggs from the witch and she hurried back to the palace.

Aoife was very angry indeed to see that her plan had again failed and she made up her mind to try once more.

Next morning she again sent Princess Noneen to the witch's cave for eggs. This time she told the girl to go by a different road, so that she wouldn't pass the blackberries.

Noneen did as Aoife told her and on the way she came to a field of wheat. She was hungry because she had not had any breakfast that morning, so she picked a handful of wheat grains and ate them.

When Noneen reached the witch's cave, the old woman asked if she had eaten anything. 'Only a handful of wheat grains,' said Noneen. 'I will have my breakfast when I go back to the palace.' Then the witch knew that her scheme had failed.

When Noneen arrived back at the palace, Aoife was so angry that she didn't say anything to her, but went out of the kitchen and up the mountain to the witch's cave.

When she reached the cave, she found the old woman sitting on a stool in the sunshine and crooning to herself.

'That was great advice you gave me,' said Aoife angrily.

'It was good advice if it had been taken properly! It wasn't my fault that the girl ate something before she reached my cave,' said the witch. 'But I will give you another plan.'

'What plan is it?' asked Aoife eagerly.

'Send her to the Well at the World's End and tell her to bring back three bottles of water from it,' said the witch. 'Nobody ever came back alive from the World's End,' she added slyly.

Aoife was delighted with this plan and as soon as she could, she spoke to Noneen about it.

'If we could only get some water from the Well at the World's End,' she said, 'our cattle and sheep would thrive as they've never done before. But what is the use of thinking about it?' she added with a sigh. 'Only a princess can get it and I don't know any princess who would be brave enough to go.'

'I'd be brave enough to go, and I am a princess,' said Noneen. 'Give me some bottles and I'll fill them from the Well at the World's End.'

So Noneen set out for the World's End.

On the first day of her journey, when she sat down to eat her breakfast, a little bird came up beside her and said, 'Will you give me the crumbs that drop from your napkin, please? I am very hungry.'

'Yes, indeed,' said Noneen, 'and more as well. Sit down and share my breakfast with me.'

The bird ate half of Noneen's breakfast and when they had finished there was not as much as a crumb left.

When Noneen was ready to set out on her journey again, the bird said: 'You will come to a field of briars which will cut and hurt you unless you have a charm against their power. If you tear a slit in the hem of your cloak, you will come safely through,' he said, and with these words he flew away.

Noneen continued her journey, and after a while the sun grew very warm and she sat down to rest.

'It must be nearly dinner-time,' she said to herself, 'for I feel hungry.' And she took out the little packet of bread which Aoife had given her for her dinner.

As she began to eat it, a tiny little woman came up to her and said, 'Will you give me the crumbs that drop from your napkin, please? I am very hungry.'

'Yes, indeed,' said Noneen, 'and more as well. Sit down and share my dinner with me.'

Noneen and the little woman ate all the bread, and when they had finished the little woman said, 'You will come to a field of glass and it will be very hard to cross it unless you wear these slippers.' And she handed Noneen a sweet little pair of slippers.

Noneen thanked her and started again on her journey. After walking for a long time, she sat down to take her supper. A tiny little man came up beside her and said, 'Will you give me the crumbs that drop from your napkin, please? I am very hungry.'

'Yes, indeed,' said Noneen, 'and more as well. Sit down and share my supper with me.'

The little man sat down and shared Noneen's supper with her.

When they had finished he said to her, 'You will come to a field of wild animals, but if you hold up this magic wand before them, they will let you pass unharmed.'

The princess thanked the little man and went on her journey again. She came to the field of briars and thorns, but when she tore a slit in the hem of her cloak the briars and the thorns parted and made a clear passage for her, and she walked straight through.

She went along till she came to the field of glass. She put on the glass slippers and walked across as easily as if she were crossing a level road. Later she came to the field of wild beasts. They were very fierce and savage and it seemed as if they would devour her, but when she held up the magic wand the lion rubbed his big head against her feet, the wolf licked her hand, and they were all as gentle and as quiet as lambs. She walked through the field and arrived at the World's End.

Now, at the Well at the World's End there were three little men.

'I wish, I wish,' said the first.

'What do you wish?' asked the others.

'I wish,' said the first, 'that beautiful as Noneen is this year, she will be three times more beautiful next year.'

'I wish, I wish,' said the second.

'What do you wish?' asked the others.

'I wish,' said the second, 'that every time she combs her hair she will comb a bag of gold out of one side and a bag of silver out of the other.'

'I wish, I wish,' said the third.

'What do you wish?' asked the others.

'I wish,' said the third, 'that all the nobles and gentlemen of the land will be seeking to marry her.'

Each of the three little men filled a bottle of the World's End water for Noneen, and she returned home.

Aoife was furious when she saw that Princess Noneen had arrived home safely and she was angrier still when she saw that Noneen was more beautiful than ever and that she could have gold and silver whenever she wished, just by combing her hair.

That very day all the rich and noble princes of the land came and asked for Princess Noneen's hand in marriage. This made Aoife so angry that she hurried out of the palace and up to the witch's cave.

'What do you mean by allowing Noneen to come back from the World's End?' she asked the witch.

'Well,' said the witch with a sly smile, 'now that the king's daughter has done so well, would you not think of sending Maeve to the World's End?'

Aoife thought this was a wonderful plan. It wouldn't matter whether she got rid of Noneen or not, if her own Maeve could have the same rich gifts.

Next morning Aoife prepared some nice food for her daughter and sent her off to the World's End.

When Maeve sat down to eat her breakfast, the little bird that Noneen had met came up beside her.

'Will you give me the crumbs which drop from your napkin?' asked the bird. 'I am very hungry.'

'No, indeed, I won't. Go away, you nasty little bird,' said Maeve.

Well, of course, Maeve did not get the warning to tear a slit in her cloak. She went along and later on she sat down to take her dinner. Along came the little woman that Noneen had met.

'Will you give me the crumbs that drop from your napkin, please? I am very hungry.'

'Get away, you nasty thing,' said Maeve.

She did not get the glass slippers, either. She went

on her journey and when evening came she sat down to take her supper. Up came the little man.

'Will you give me the crumbs that drop from your napkin, please? I am very hungry.'

'Get away,' said Maeve. 'You will get nothing from me.' Of course she did not get the wand. She came to the field of briars. The thorns and brambles tore and cut her and made her face and hands very sore. She came to the field of glass and fell and slipped many times, so that it was with the greatest difficulty she was able to get across.

She came to the field of wild beasts, and only that a fierce bull caught her on his horns and hurled her over the fence, she would have been torn to pieces by the savage animals. At last she reached the Well at the World's End and saw the three little men sitting there.

'I wish, I wish,' said the first.

'What do you wish?' asked the others.

'I wish,' said the first, 'that ugly as Maeve is this year, she will be three times uglier next year.'

'I wish, I wish,' said the second.

'What do you wish?' asked the others.

'I wish,' said the second, 'that every time she combs her hair she will comb a bag of soot out of one side and a bag of ashes out of the other.'

'I wish, I wish,' said the third.

'What do you wish?' asked the others.

'I wish,' said the third, 'that all the robbers and

villains of the land will want to marry her.'

Maeve arrived home safely, and at first her mother was glad to see her. Then she noticed that she was uglier than ever and when the girl combed her hair soot and ashes came out instead of the gold and silver she expected. This made her very angry indeed, but when every villain and wicked man in the land came to the palace to ask for Maeve's hand in marriage, Aoife was still more annoyed.

She again visited the witch of Grass Mountain and the wicked old woman told her she had one more plan for getting rid of Noneen.

'In yonder castle there lives a giant,' she said, pointing to a huge castle that stood on the side of the mountain. 'If you send Princess Noneen over there, she will never come back alive.'

Next day Aoife asked Noneen to take some cakes over to the giant's castle as a present.

As she watched the princess walking down the road with the basketful of cakes on her arm, she smiled a wicked smile. 'That's the end of you, my girl,' she said.

There was nobody at the giant's castle when Noneen arrived. She went into the kitchen. It was very dirty and untidy. She lighted the fire, swept the floor, and put everything in order. She heard the giant coming home. When he came in and saw her, he looked fierce, but when he glanced round the kitchen he was pleased to see how clean and bright it was. A dog was sitting at one side of the fire and a cat at the other.

'Go away,' said the giant. 'Go away or I will kill you.'

'Oh, wait till I feed the cat,' said Noneen.

The giant watched her while she fed the cat. Then: 'Go away, go away,' he said again, 'for no one ever leaves this house alive.'

'Oh, wait till I feed the dog,' said Noneen. She was so kind and gentle that, instead of killing her, he gave her a present of gold and jewels and sent her home.

Princess Noneen came back to the palace that evening with all the jewels and gold which the giant had given her. Aoife was very angry and very jealous when she saw her and made up her mind to send Maeve to the giant's castle next day.

Next morning Aoife sent her own daughter to the giant's castle. Instead of cleaning the kitchen, she sat down with her feet in the ashes, and she put the dog and cat outside the door.

The giant came home. He looked at her and said, 'Clean the kitchen.'

'Indeed, I will not,' she replied.

'Feed the dog,' said the giant.

'Indeed, I will not feed the ugly brute,' said Maeve.

'Feed the cat.'

'Indeed, he may starve before I will feed him,' she said.

The giant grew very angry. He snatched up a big stick and chased her out of his castle.

The king was riding past the castle just then and he saw the giant chasing Maeve. The giant stopped running when he saw the king.

'Good evening, Your Highness,' said he.

'Good evening, Giant,' said the King, 'and why are you chasing poor Maeve?'

Then the giant told the king of all the evil deeds of Maeve and her mother. He had heard of them from his brother, who had lived near the World's End.

The king was very angry and he banished both of them from his kingdom.

Princess Noneen and her father were very happy together, and one day Noneen married a great and good prince, and her father lived happily with her and her husband and children.

The Wig and the Wag

Once upon a time there was a woman and she had three daughters. The two elder girls, Niamh and Mella, were lazy and idle, but the youngest, Nuala, was good and industrious and very kind to her mother.

One day Niamh said to herself, 'I am tired of being here. I will go and seek my fortune.' She told her mother of her plan and she agreed and said, 'All right, go to the well and get a pitcher of water, and I will bake a cake for you to take on your journey.'

So the girl went to the well to fill her pitcher, and at the well there was a bird, which said:

'Fill it with moss and line it with clay,
And you'll carry your pitcherful all away.'

'Get away,' said Niamh. 'Why should I put moss and clay into my pitcher?'

But foolish Niamh did not know there was a hole in the pitcher, and by the time she got home there was very little water left in it, and her mother could make only a very small cake.

When the cake was ready her mother said, 'Which will you have, the half of the cake with my blessing or the whole of it without my blessing?'

'Oh,' said Niamh, 'it would not be worth while dividing such a small cake as that. I will take the whole of it without your blessing.'

Niamh went off to seek her fortune without her mother's blessing. She walked on and on and at last she came to a house in a lonely part of a woods. She knocked at the door and it was answered by a little old woman.

'Do you want anyone to help you to do the work of the house?' asked Niamh.

'Yes,' said the woman. 'I do. Now, you can do all the housework, but there is one thing about which I want to warn you. Never look up the chimney. If you do, something will fall down and kill you.'

The old woman had stolen a bag of money from the house of a rich man who lived some distance from the woods and had hidden this bag of money in the chimney. One day the old woman went out. Niamh was very inquisitive and the first thing she did was to look up the chimney. Down fell a big bag of money. She took the money and ran from the house as fast as she could.

She met a cow on the road and the cow said, 'Oh, will you milk me? I have not been milked these seven years.'

'Indeed,' said Niamh, 'I have no time to milk you.'

She started off again and further on she came to a horse.

'Oh,' said the horse, 'will you ride me? I have not been ridden these seven years.'

'Indeed, I won't,' said Niamh. 'I am in a hurry.' And she walked off.

Then she came to a mill.

'Oh,' said the mill, 'will you grind me? I have not been ground these seven years.'

'Indeed, I won't,' said Niamh. She sat down behind the mill to count the money.

The old woman came home and found that the girl had gone. Then she looked up the chimney and saw that the money had gone also. She went off as quickly as she could to try to find the girl. She came to the cow and said:

> 'Cow o' mine, cow o' thine,
> Did you e'er see a fair maid o' mine,
> With the wig, with the wag,
> With the long leathern bag,

> More money than ever I had,
> Since I was a young maid,
> And now I'm an old hag?'

'Follow on before you,' said the cow and off she went again. She came to the horse.

> 'Horse o' mine, horse o' thine,
> Did you e'er see a fair maid o' mine,
> With the wig, with the wag,
> With the long leathern bag,
> More money than ever I had,
> Since I was a young maid,
> And now I'm an old hag?'

'Follow on before you,' said the horse.
   'I will,' said the old woman and off she went. She came to the mill.

> 'Mill o' mine, mill o' thine,
> Did you e'er see a fair maid o' mine,
> With the wig, with the wag,
> With the long leathern bag,
> More money than ever I had,
> Since I was a young maid,
> And now I'm an old hag?'

'Here behind me,' said the mill. The old woman found Niamh sitting behind the mill, counting the money.

'Ha, you bold girl! I've caught you at last! Give me my bag of money or it will be the worse for you,' she said, and, lifting her stick, she gave Niamh a good beating. Then she hurried home with the bag of money on her back, and left Niamh feeling very sorry for herself.

Now, the second daughter, Mella, said to her mother that she, too, would go to seek her fortune. She went to the well, and, like Niamh, she refused the advice of the bird and left home without her mother's blessing. She had in every way the same experience as her elder sister.

She took the bag of money and on her way home met the cow and the horse and the mill, just as Niamh did. She refused to help them, and when the old woman found her bag of money had gone, she didn't have much trouble in finding Mella.

When she caught up with the girl, she took the bag of money from her, and after giving her a good beating with her stick, she hurried home.

At last, the youngest daughter, Nuala, said to her mother that she, too, would go to seek her fortune.

'Very well,' said the mother, 'go to the well for a pitcher of water, and I will make you a cake to take with you on your journey.'

So the girl went to the well. The little bird was there and said to her, as he had said to Niamh and Mella:

'Fill it with moss and line it with clay,
And you'll carry your pitcherful all away.'

'Thank you,' said the girl, 'I will.' And she put some moss and clay into the pitcher, and when she went home her hand was very tired from carrying the big, full pitcher. Her mother made her a great big cake, and said:

'Now, which will you have, the half of the cake with my blessing or the whole of it without my blessing?'

'Oh, Mother!' said the girl, 'I will take half the cake, for I would not like to leave home without your blessing.'

The mother cut the cake in two, gave half to the girl and she blessed her. Nuala then set out on her journey. One evening she came to the house in the woods. The old woman said she would take her in to do all the work.

'But,' she said, 'there were two girls here lately who did not do what I told them, and I hope now that you will. You can do anything you like in the house except look up the chimney.'

The old woman went out, and the girl cleaned the house. She went to the fire to put on the potatoes for the dinner. While she was fixing the pot on the fire she bent over, and in turning her head, without meaning to do it, she glanced up the chimney. Down fell the bag of money. Now, Nuala had heard that a bag of money had been stolen from a certain rich man and she thought this must be it. She took the bag and hurried away to restore it to the proper owner. She came to the cow.

'Oh,' said the cow, 'will you milk me? I have not been milked these seven years.'

'Oh, well,' said Nuala, 'I am in a hurry, but still I will have pity on you.' So she milked the cow and then went on her way.

Later she came to the horse, who said, 'Oh, will you please ride me, young girl? I have not been ridden these seven years.'

'Yes,' said Nuala, 'though I am in a hurry, I will ride you.' And she rode the horse around and around before she continued her journey.

That evening she came to the mill.

'Oh, please, will you grind me? I have not been ground these seven years!' said the mill, and Nuala did so. After she had ground the mill, Nuala sat down behind it to count the money.

The old woman came home, missed the money, and hurried off to find Nuala. She came to the cow.

> 'Cow o' mine, cow o' thine,
> Did you e'er see a fair maid o' mine,
> With the wig, with the wag,
> With the long leathern bag,

> More money than ever I had,
> Since I was a young maid,
> And now I'm an old hag?'

The cow caught her on its horns and tossed her in the air. She was very bruised and hurt, but still she continued her journey. Later on she came to the horse.

> 'Horse o' mine, horse o' thine,
> Did you e'er see a fair maid o' mine,
> With the wig, with the wag,
> With the long leathern bag,
> More money than ever I had,
> Since I was a young maid,
> And now I'm an old hag?'

The horse tried to kick her and chased her away. She kept on running till she came to the mill.

> 'Mill o' mine, mill o' thine,
> Did you e'er see a fair maid o' mine,
> With the wig, with the wag,
> With the long leathern bag,
> More money than ever I had,
> Since I was a young maid,
> And now I'm an old hag?'

The mill-wheel ground her into pieces.

The girl went home, and she and her mother went

to the house of the rich man to give him the bag of money. He thanked them, but said he had plenty of money without what was in the leathern bag.

'Please take it as a gift,' he said to Nuala. 'Your honesty deserves a reward.'

He then asked Nuala if she would marry him, and if she and her mother would come to live in his grand house.

Nuala said she would like to marry him and she did, and they all lived happily ever after.

Eagle and Angel

Once upon a time there was a rich man and woman who had a beautiful daughter. She was so beautiful that they called her Angel.

One day the man was out hunting. He climbed up a mountain and found an eagle's nest. He expected to find the eggs of some little eaglets there, but, to his surprise, he found a little boy. He took the child out of the nest, wrapped him carefully in a huge scarf and climbed down to the foot of the mountain. When he reached home he told his wife of his adventure and showed her the child.

'Let's keep him and bring him up with our little girl,' he said.

'Indeed, yes,' said his wife, 'and because you found him in an eagle's nest, we'll call him Eagle.' So Eagle the little boy was called from that day.

Eagle and Angel grew up together and they thought for a long while that they were brother and sister. When they grew up someone told them how Eagle had come to the house, and they loved each other so much that they decided to marry.

The father and mother did not want their daughter to marry so soon and they made up their minds to get Eagle out of the house. They sent for a witch who lived near them and asked her what was the best plan to get rid of the boy. The witch told them to leave a cauldron of boiling lead outside the house that evening when Eagle would be returning home, and that he would walk into it in the dusk and be burned to death.

Now none of the three of them knew that Angel was lying on her bed in the next room and that she heard the whole plot.

When Eagle was coming home in the evening, Angel was at her window, watching for him. As he came toward the house, she called out to him, 'Don't come any farther! Stay where you are.'

She threw out to him a bundle of her clothes and jewels and as many precious things as she could collect, and along with these the witch's wand which she had managed to get, unknown to the witch.

When she managed to get outside, she told Eagle how they were plotting against him.

'Now,' she said, 'we'll have to run away, for they'll try some other trick since this one didn't work.'

They started off on their journey and after they had been travelling for some time Angel said to Eagle, 'Look behind and see if there is anyone coming.'

Eagle looked behind and said, 'The trees are shaking and the dust is flying, and I see two men not very far off.'

'These,' said Angel, 'must be men coming to look for us.'

'Ah!' exclaimed Eagle. 'They will take you from me.'

'Oh, no,' said Angel, and with the witch's wand she changed Eagle into a bear and herself into an old man. She got on the bear's back and kept riding on.

Up came the two men. 'Did you see a boy and girl passing along here?' they asked the old man.

'No,' said the old man, 'no boy and girl passed by here while I have been riding.'

'Well,' said one man to the other, 'I think we had better go home as we cannot find them.'

They returned home and found the father, mother and the witch waiting for them.

'Well,' said the witch, 'did you see them?'

'Indeed we did not,' they replied. 'All we saw was an old man riding on a bear, and the old man told us that no boy nor girl had passed along the way.'

'That old man was Angel,' said the witch, 'and the bear was Eagle. You had better go off again in the morning and see if you can find them.'

The next day the two men started off again.

Angel said to Eagle, 'Look behind and see if there is anyone coming.'

'The trees are shaking and the dust is flying and I see two men not very far off,' said Eagle.

'These,' said Angel, 'are two men coming to look for us.'

'Ah,' said Eagle, 'they will take you from me.'

'Oh, no,' said Angel.

With the witch's wand she turned Eagle into a bed of moss and she turned herself into a bee humming on the moss.

Up came the two men.

'I am tired,' said one to the other. 'Let us rest on this nice, soft moss for a while.'

The men lay down on the moss but the bee kept stinging them, stinging them. They got up and one of them put a handful of the soft green moss in his pocket. They returned home and found the father, mother and witch waiting for them.

'Did you see Eagle and Angel?' said the witch.

'No, indeed. We went as far as a bed of moss and lay down to rest but a bee kept stinging us.'

'You did see them,' said the witch, 'for that bee was Angel and the moss you have in your pocket is a bit of Eagle's hair. You and I,' she said to the father and mother, 'will go after them ourselves tomorrow.'

The next morning the witch and the father and mother got a jaunting car and started on their journey.

Angel and Eagle were still travelling and were about to sit down and rest when Angel said to Eagle, 'Look behind and see if there is anyone coming.'

'The trees are shaking and the dust is flying and I see a jaunting car not very far off,' answered Eagle.

'These,' said Angel, 'are my father and mother and the witch coming to look for us.'

'Ah,' said Eagle, 'they will surely take you from me now.'

'No, have no fear,' said Angel.

She turned Eagle into a pond and herself into a duck swimming on the pond.

Up came the jaunting car.

'Now,' said the witch, 'here they are.'

The witch went over to the edge of the pond and said, 'My pretty little duck and my handsome little duck, will you come to me now?'

'No,' said the duck, 'I won't come till you give me the golden box you have in your pocket.'

'Oh,' said the witch, 'I wouldn't give the box to anyone.'

'Well,' said the duck, 'I won't come to you till I get it.'

'Here it is, then,' said the witch and she threw it out to her.

The duck took the golden box in her beak, dived to

the bottom of the pond and left it below. She came up again and began swimming on the pond.

'My pretty little duck and my handsome little duck, will you come to me now?' said the witch.

'No,' said the duck, 'I won't come till you give me the golden ball in your pocket.'

'Oh,' said the witch, 'I wouldn't give the golden ball to anyone.'

'Well then, I won't come till I get the golden ball.'

'Here it is, then,' said the witch and she threw her the golden ball.

The duck took the golden ball in her beak, dived to the bottom of the pond and left it below. She rose to the surface again and began swimming about. Again the witch said:

'My pretty little duck and my handsome little duck, will you come to me now?'

The duck flew up out of the water with the witch's wand in her beak and turned her father, mother, the witch and the jaunting car into a milestone. She then changed herself and Eagle into their own shapes and they began their travels again.

Now as Eagle went along, the place seemed familiar to him. He felt he had been there before. At last he arrived at a house and suddenly he knew it was his father's house. He told Angel this. But she was frightened and said, 'If you go in there, you will forget me.'

'No,' said Eagle, 'I will never forget you.'

'Listen,' said Angel, 'don't let anyone kiss you, because if you do, you will forget me. I will wait for you here in this tree. I will climb up amongst the branches and wait till you come, but if you let anyone kiss you, you will forget me.'

Eagle went into the house. His father, mother, brothers and sisters and all his friends were delighted to see him, because they had thought him surely lost. They crowded around him and tried to kiss him, but he would not let any one of them come near him. He sat down at the fire and at last the little lap-dog jumped up and kissed him, and he forgot poor Angel.

The tree in which Angel was waiting stood over a well. A blacksmith's daughter who lived close by came to fill her pitcher at the well. She leaned over and saw the reflection of the beautiful face in the water.

'Oh!' said she. 'Such a lovely girl as I am to be a blacksmith's daughter!'

She broke her pitcher and went off to seek her fortune.

Next day the blacksmith's wife came to fill a can at the well. She looked into the water and saw the beautiful face.

'Oh!' said she. 'Such a lovely woman as I am to be a blacksmith's wife!'

She threw away her can and went off to seek her fortune.

The next day the poor blacksmith himself came to the well. He had no vessel to bring but an old saucepan. When he looked into the water, he said, 'That is not a man's face.'

He gazed and gazed and at last he looked up the tree and saw Angel.

'Come down here at once,' he ordered, 'you who sent my daughter and my wife away, and are now trying to send myself. Come down till I kill you.'

Poor Angel came down trembling, but when the blacksmith saw how beautiful she was and how gentle, he could not kill or hurt her. Instead, he got her into Eagle's house as a servant.

Now when Angel went into the house, what did she find but that Eagle was going to be married the next day. The night before the wedding there was a great feast and all the guests were gathered round a big table. Eagle was seated beside the girl he was going to marry. Each person had to sing a song, tell a story or give a riddle.

When it came Angel's turn, she said, 'I can't sing a song, tell a story or give a riddle but I will do something which will please you better.'

She took from her pocket the golden box and the golden ball. Out of the golden box fell two grains of wheat and out of the golden ball jumped a cock and hen. The cock picked up his own grain and the hen's grain as well.

Angel looked at Eagle and said, 'That is not the way I served you when I saved you from the cauldron of boiling lead.'

Eagle looked at her but could not remember anything.

Angel let fall two more grains of wheat and the cock picked up his own grain and the hen's grain as well.

Again Angel looked at Eagle and said, 'That is not the way I served you when I left my father and mother and home and came away with you.'

Still Eagle could not remember. Angel let fall two more grains and again the cock picked up his own grain and the hen's grain.

Angel said, 'That is not the way I served you when I turned my father and mother and the witch into a milestone.' Suddenly Eagle remembered all. He left his place beside the other girl, came to Angel, and kissed her.

Next day they had a great wedding feast, for Eagle and Angel were married and if they didn't live happily ever after, that may we.

Ashapelt

Jn the olden days, long, long ago, there lived a woman who had three daughters.

Brona and Sheila, the two elder girls, were very beautiful but the youngest was greatly disfigured, for her face was covered with hair. Her sisters were ashamed of her, though she was the cleverest of the three. They called her Ashapelt because they kept her cleaning up the ashes and cinders and doing all the hard work.

At last the elder girls determined to go away to seek their fortune. They did not wish Ashapelt to know they were going, but she overheard part of their conversation and found out what they intended to do. She determined to follow them.

Brona and Sheila rose early one morning and set

out on their journey. They were just about to sit down by the wayside and eat the dinner which they had brought with them, when they saw Ashapelt close behind them.

'Oh, what shall we do with her?' said one to the other.

They saw some men digging potatoes in a field close by. They waited till the men went to their dinner and then they took poor Ashapelt and buried her in the potato field.

Off they started again. After a while the men came back and noticed the clay moving and shifting.

'What is that?' said one of them. 'Is it a rat?'

'No,' said another of the men, 'a rat could not move like that.'

'Well,' said another, 'we will see what it is.' They began to dig and soon found Ashapelt in the clay.

'Oh, my poor girl!' exclaimed one of the men. 'Who buried you in the clay?'

'My sisters did,' said Ashapelt, 'but don't delay me now. Let me go till I catch up with them.'

Off she went and just as her sisters were about to eat their supper, they saw her close behind them.

'Oh, what shall we do with her?' asked Brona.

'Let us bind her hands and feet and tie her to this tall tree,' said Sheila. This they did and hurried off, leaving poor Ashapelt bound fast to the tree.

After a time a man came by and saw her.

'Oh, my poor girl!' he cried, 'who has left you like this?'

'My sisters,' said Ashapelt. 'But please don't delay me now, as I want to catch up with them.'

'All right,' said the man, 'and take this knife; it may be useful to you some day.'

Ashapelt thanked him and hurried off. By this time Brona and Sheila had arrived at the king's palace. Just as they were about to enter the grounds, they saw Ashapelt close behind them.

'Oh, here she is again,' said they. 'What shall we do with her?'

At last they asked her to go and stay in a little hut in the woods close by, while they went to the palace to look for service there. They promised to send for her when they were settled at their work. Days passed and Ashapelt heard nothing from her sisters, so she went to the palace, and who should be coming out of the door but the king himself. He looked at her and asked her what she wanted.

'I want my two sisters, Your Majesty,' she said.

'Who are your sisters?' asked the king.

'The two girls who came here the other day looking for work in the palace.'

'Surely,' said the king, 'these two beautiful girls are not sisters of yours.'

'They are, Your Majesty,' said Ashapelt.

The king sent for the two girls and they had to

admit that Ashapelt was their sister. They told the king that, though she had such a strange appearance, she was very clever.

'Very well,' said he, 'I shall find work for her.'

Now near the palace lived an evil old witch who had stolen some valuable things from the king. Amongst these was a wonderful lantern shaped like a half-moon. She had also stolen the king's joy bells and a small, richly worked carpet of great worth. The witch was so cunning and so wicked that no one would venture to go near her.

Ashapelt had been in the palace for some time, working in the kitchen, when the king sent for her.

'Look here,' said he, 'I will marry my eldest son to your eldest sister if you get for me the half-moon that the witch stole from me.'

'That I'll do,' said Ashapelt, 'if you give me a bag of salt.'

Ashapelt got the bag of salt. One very dark night she went to the witch's house with it. She knocked at the door.

'Who's there?' asked the witch.

'Oh,' said Ashapelt, 'it is very dark and cold and will you please let me sit at the fire till morning?'

Now though the witch was so wicked, she would not break the custom of giving shelter for the night to a lonely traveller. She let Ashapelt in and told her to sit down by the fire. The witch was making porridge for her supper. She put salt and meal into the water. Ashapelt waited till she turned away from the fire and then she herself put three handfuls of salt into the porridge. When it was cooked the witch gave her some.

'Oh, ma'am,' said Ashapelt, 'I can't eat this porridge. There is too much salt in it.'

'I put only a little salt in it,' said the witch.

'Well, taste it please, ma'am,' said Ashapelt.

'It is far too salty,' said the witch, 'but I can't make any more porridge now, for there is not a drop of water in the house.'

'Will you lend me the half-moon I see there in the corner, and I will go to the well for water?'

'Indeed I won't,' said the witch. 'I would not let anyone but myself handle that half-moon.'

'Well,' said Ashapelt, 'will you take the half-moon and give me the can, and we will go to the well?'

Ashapelt and the witch went to the well. When they reached it, Ashapelt said, 'I don't know how to get the water from the well. I will hold the half-moon and you can take the can.'

The witch gave her the half-moon and stooped over the water. Ashapelt darted off. When the witch turned round after filling the can, she saw Ashapelt running away with the half-moon. She dropped the can and followed her so swiftly that she had almost caught up with her, when Ashapelt came to a stream, over which she jumped quickly for she knew that no witch can cross running water.

There was great joy in the palace when the half-moon was restored to the king.

Wedding preparations immediately began and Brona and the eldest prince were married shortly after.

A few weeks later the king again summoned Ashapelt to his presence.

'Now,' said he, 'I will marry my second eldest son to your second eldest sister, if you get me the joy bells the witch stole from me.'

'That I'll do, Your Majesty,' said Ashapelt, 'if you get me a bag of wool.'

Ashapelt got the bag of wool. She had found out that the witch had the joy bells in the stable, where she kept a donkey, which brayed loudly when anyone entered. Ashapelt got a bunch of fresh carrots and when she came to the door of the stable, she threw them to the donkey. He immediately began to feast on them and while he was eating, Ashapelt stuffed the bells with wool. She then ran out quickly, and when she had passed the witch's house, she removed the wool so that the bells rang out clearly on the still night air. The witch ran after her in fury, and was just catching up with her, when she reached the stream which the witch could not cross.

Again, there was great rejoicing in the palace, and Sheila's marriage with the second eldest prince was even more magnificent than Brona's had been.

A few weeks later the king again sent for Ashapelt.

'Now,' said he, 'I will marry my youngest son to you, yourself, if you get for me the carpet which the witch has stolen.'

The youngest prince, Prince Connla, was noble and handsome, and beloved by everyone.

'Well, Your Majesty,' said Ashapelt, 'as I have done so much for my sisters, I had better do something for myself.'

Ashapelt waited till one day she saw the witch going out to gather firewood. She then slipped into the house and crept under the bed. She saw that the witch used the carpet as a quilt.

When night came and the witch was sound asleep, and snoring loudly, Ashapelt gave the carpet a chuck. The witch stirred in her sleep and pulled the carpet back. Ashapelt waited a while and gave the carpet another chuck. The witch gave it a chuck. Ashapelt gave it another chuck. The witch gave it another chuck. At last Ashapelt chucked so hard that she pulled the carpet with her under the bed. Out jumped the witch and pulled Ashapelt from under the bed.

'Oh! you wretch!' she cried. 'I have you at last, you who stole my half-moon, my joy bells and who are now trying to steal my carpet. Now tell me,' she continued, 'if anyone treated you in this manner, what death would you give them?'

Ashapelt thought for a moment.

'Well, ma'am,' said she, 'I would put her in a sack and tie the sack up the chimney. Then I would go to the woods and get a big stick and I would beat her, beat her, beat her till she was dead.'

'That is the very death you will get,' said the witch.

She tied Ashapelt in a sack, put the sack up the chimney, and ran off to the woods to get a big, heavy stick.

When she was gone Ashapelt cut the sack open with the knife she had been given by the man who had loosened her bonds when she was tied to the tree. She then got another sack and filled it with stones, after which she hurried back to the palace with the carpet.

The witch delayed in the woods, seeking for a very heavy stick. When she finally returned home, she took down the sack.

'Hah! Hah!' she said, 'you have got heavy since I put you up there.'

She began to hit the sack as hard as ever she could.

'Hah! Hah!' she said, 'your bones are cracking.' She kept beating, beating for a long time. When at last she opened the sack and saw what was inside, her rage and disappointment were so great that her heart stopped beating and she fell dead.

The king was delighted to get back his carpet, but when he asked Connla to take Ashapelt for his wife, the young prince refused.

'Father,' he said, 'I could not marry a girl with a face like that.'

'What shall I do?' said the king. 'I cannot break my royal word.'

The queen was present.

'I have a plan,' said she. 'Connla is celebrated for his wonderful dancing and I believe Ashapelt is equally so. Have a fire lighted and let them both dance in front of it. Whoever can dance nearest to the fire without being scorched or burned will have the choice to marry or not.'

A great fire was lighted in an open space. Connla and Ashapelt danced before it for a long time, until at last Ashapelt stumbled and would have fallen into the flames if the prince had not caught her. A spark lighted on her face and burned off the hair, leaving her much more beautiful than either of her sisters.

The prince fell on his knees and begged her to marry him. The wedding took place almost immediately. It lasted seven days and seven nights, and among all the ladies, no one was half as beautiful as Connla's lovely bride, Ashapelt.

The End